TACK & jibe

a novel

LILAH SUZANNE

interlude  press • new york

ISBN 13: 978-1-945053-93-1 (trade)
ISBN 13: 978-1-945053-94-8 (ebook)
Published by Interlude Press
http://interludepress.com
This is a work of fiction. Names, characters, and places are either a product
of the author's imagination or are used fictitiously. Any resemblance
to real persons, either living or dead, is entirely coincidental.
BOOK AND COVER DESIGN BY CB Messer
10 9 8 7 6 5 4 3 2 1

interlude press • new york

"The glitter of sunlight on roughened water, the glory of the stars, the innocence of morning, the smell of the sea in harbors, the feathery blur and smoky buddings of young boughs, and something there that comes and goes and never can be captured, the thorn of spring, the sharp and tongueless cry—these things will always be the same."

—Thomas Wolfe

CH. *1*

WILLA ROGERS WAKES TO THE mournful bellow of the Porter Island ferry. She swings her legs to the floor, the ever-present sand gritty on the soles of her feet, and rises from bed right on schedule. Her bosses at Porter Sails don't mind if she's late—island time and all—and she's never had much use for an alarm. Thanks to the clockwork timing of the ferry blaring when it picks up commuters to take them to coastal North Carolina's mainland, Willa couldn't oversleep if she tried.

Her roommate Bodhi is still blissfully snoring away, twisted in the sheets on the lower bunk bed in her room with long sandy-colored hair flopped messily over her face. Willa plucks her phone from the charging port beneath the TV stand, pours a bowl of dry cereal and a glass of the combined last dregs of three different Gatorade bottles, and scrolls through Instagram. She's already showered and dressed in board shorts, a long-sleeved T-shirt, and her favorite worn Vans when Bodhi finds her leaning out over the railing as far as she can, on the upstairs deck.

"Don't jump," Bodhi says, then yawns and stretches leisurely. "Or do. Whatever."

Willa locks her feet more securely around a post and doesn't take Bodhi's lack of concern for her safety personally; even if she *was* going to jump—or fall, more likely—the house sits on soft, gray sand and swishing patches of sea grass and is two whole stories of charming beach cottage or one whole story raised on stilts. The open garage below stores Bodhi's jumble of outdoor equipment: tents and a kayak and a fishing boat, her bicycle and fishing gear and mud-crusted hiking boots. Neither of them has a car; the island is small enough that it's not necessary. And when summer vacationers take over the cottage, Bodhi's equipment becomes part of the vacation package. Porter Island is small and rural and only accessible via ferry or boat and appeals to those who like to consider themselves outdoorsy, but only for a week or so.

"I'm running out of morning-view shots." Willa aims her phone camera through the branches of a loblolly tree, hoping to catch a shot of clear blue sky contrasted against an unfocused cluster of shiny green leaves. In the spring and summer, the tree is speckled with fat, snowy white flowers but in the chill of late October the tree is decidedly uninspiring.

"Here's your morning view," Bodhi says and flips her the bird.

Willa climbs down from the railing and pockets her phone. As they go inside, she comments, "I doubt that'll go over very well," though Bodhi's sun-freckled beach-bum look could be almost tailor-made for Instagram, if she cared about such a thing.

She's known Bodhi for five years now, since just before Willa started working after high school at the newly opened sailing store that Bodhi's parents own. For nine months out of the year they share Willa's grandparents' beach cottage—from the day after Labor Day until the end of May—and for the other three, Willa couch surfs and borrows patches of floor and Bodhi camps or sails wherever the wind blows her in a sturdy little sailboat for one. Bodhi, for the most part, does what she wants, funded by her parents, as do most of the young adults stuck on this island. Willa has had to be responsible for herself since before she even knew what that word meant.

"Are you going to the store today?" Bodhi asks while standing in front of the open fridge door. The contents are sparse as Bodhi's holey T-shirt and sweatpants.

"I guess I could," Willa says, hoping her tone conveys how very much she does not want to do that.

"Nah, it's cool." Bodhi scrapes grape jelly onto a tortilla, pours cereal on top, and then rolls it up like a burrito. Bodhi can't be bothered to do regular grocery shopping, but since she's the only one who pays her own rent, Willa can't afford much shopping and she can't let Bodhi know that *her* simple beach-bum lifestyle is by necessity, not choice. No one is funding Willa's cereal-and-jelly burritos.

Willa fishes in the change jar on the counter. She comes up with enough money for an actual breakfast and grabs her keys from the fake-seashell key hook and her skateboard from the porch. "I'm going by The Sand Dollar. I'll pick you up something."

"That's cool," Bodhi says, her mouth full of jelly-and-cereal burrito, providing an answer that's neither affirmative nor negative but standard for her.

Willa winds through the flat streets of Porter Island with her curly hair flying behind her and the cool autumn air making her eyes water. She glides out of their neighborhood, where the little cottages with cedar shake siding in soft grays and blues and browns and greens are made to blend in with the surrounding trees and sand, then on to the streets closer to the shore where stately beach houses and upscale resorts are painted in bold pastels to stand out dramatically against the pale sky. The resort areas are quiet now in the off season; tourist activity is down to a trickle until spring break comes around again and changes the fabric of the town from quiet little beach town to vacation hot spot.

At the main road Willa guides her board up onto the sidewalk where the row of beach-side businesses starts. She rolls past The Oyster Bar and a waterfront seafood restaurant, a vintage, family-owned motel, a bike rental shop and a hammock store. There's a gas station and a tiny hardware store and an overpriced general store with only the bare basics at jacked up prices. A big grocery store at normal prices is a ferry ride and car rental, another reason not to bother. The ocean comes into clear view, choppy today, a moody dark blue with white-capped waves.

She glides past a clutch of shops, a pier, and a hot dog stand down to a marina where sailboats sway and flutter like butterflies perched on the sea. Next to the marina and down a white-stone path is where the sea-shanty-looking Porter Sails has set up shop.

Willa detours right, curving around the southern tip of the island past the nicer hotels and shops and slows to a stop at The Sand Dollar Cafe. She orders a breakfast sandwich for Bodhi to have whenever she happens to swan into work and a pumpkin spice latte for herself. She's not crazy about them, really, but they're a popular hashtag right now with fall in full swing. Under one arm, Willa tucks a paper bag with the sandwich inside; she juggles the open latte carefully with the other—no lid, so the foam art isn't ruined before she can get a picture. She hustles out the door already opening her camera app and hops back on her skateboard without looking at what's ahead of her. She has a perfect morning-view photo idea: the latte held up against the brooding ocean and mellow mid-morning sun with the caption "Autumn in the Outer Banks." Maybe not her best post ever, but if she picks the right hashtags and makes sure to tag both the cafe and the sail shop it should—

"Hey! Watch out!"

Willa snaps to attention, but too late; she just barely manages to avoid colliding with someone by taking a hard turn to the right—too hard. She tumbles off the board. Her pumpkin spice latte flies from her hand, lands at the feet of the person she nearly skated right into, and splashes them from knee to very expensive-looking shoe tips and, most tragically, ruins Willa's last hope for any #morningview likes and comments.

CH. 2

"UGH! ARE YOU *KIDDING* ME?"

The woman has chin-length black hair, dark eyes, and a rich alto voice. She also picked the worst possible day to wear white slacks.

"Crap." Willa scrambles up, registering a sting on her right palm and an ache on her right elbow. She collects her skateboard and the bag of food and digs inside of it to find a napkin as she approaches the woman. "Here you go." Willa extends the napkin toward her; it has some bacon grease stains and little chunk of melted cheese on it. The woman scowls at the napkin and turns away, returning to her completely ineffective method of trying to brush the huge, brown, wet spots off of her pants with her hands.

Willa shrugs, then realizes her shoulder hurts too. She hasn't taken a spill like that in quite a while. "I'll go get some clean napkins," she tries, but the woman waves that off.

"Don't bother, I'll change at my office." Disdain drips from her words. "Luckily I plan for these sorts of things since apparently half the population here spends most of their time *fucking around.*" She says the last part with a deliberate glare.

Willa frowns; that's unfair. Sure they have a decent amount of retirees who live here full time and unemployed surfers who pile by the dozens into the snug beach cottages, and, yes, most of her friends are sort of biding their time until they go to work for their parents, and Bodhi's moms *technically* pay her rent for a house that is technically not theirs, but still, that's not Willa.

"You could have moved out of the way," Willa retorts with a scowl of her own, dropping her skateboard back onto the pavement with a petulant *clack.*

"Moved out of the way? You were so busy staring at your phone you almost ran me over!" The woman's dark eyes narrow, and her chin lifts. She has sharp cheekbones and a strong jaw and dark, arched eyebrows—nice body too. She'd be hot if she wasn't such an asshole. "You could pay attention to the real world instead of getting the perfect selfie!"

Willa swallows the retort on her lips, that she wasn't taking a selfie because she only does those on Selfie Saturdays. "Yeah. Well." Willa huffs a few times for lack of a better response and finally settles on, "Sorry I ran into you or whatever."

"Yeah, me too." The woman turns on her heel and stomps out of the parking lot. Now a little shaky and out of sorts, Willa growls in frustration and hops back on her board. And she's injured. Ugh, *tourists.*

Work is quiet when Willa gets in and stays that way for the rest of the morning. She raids the first aid kit in the back office. Moving a little slower than usual with one arm bandaged up, she's alone for the entire morning. Robin and Jenn have some sort of bank business to deal with. Bodhi remains a no-show. The odds are fifty-fifty that she went back to sleep or headed over to the other side of the island to kayak in the calm, shallow waters of the sound. On her lunch break, Willa eats half of the now-cold breakfast sandwich she picked up for Bodhi. A few customers come in looking for cold weather sailing gear—waterproof Gore-Tex jackets and neoprene boots and thick rash-pants—then Willa spends the early afternoon unloading boxes of new merchandise: sailing gloves and multitools and quick-release harnesses. It takes longer than it should because Willa carries the boxes one-by-one instead of in a stack the way she usually could. After opening a box of sports watches, Willa slips an elegant, leather-banded watch on her wrist and ducks outside.

The marina next door houses the boats of residents and visitors, as well as a small stock for sale. Willa glances around and quickly boards a beautiful Marlin Heritage daysailer. She props her phone against the base of the mast, sets the timer on the camera, and carefully but quickly sits on the edge of the bow, facing out toward the water, making sure her arm with the watch is in frame and her injured arm is out of it. She quickly hops back out of the boat, already scrolling through the photos to find the best one. Crossing the gravel path back to the shop, Willa picks the perfect shot, where the sun is everywhere: a burst of light obscuring half of her body and face, bright on the polished deck of the sailboat, shining in the twists of her curls, reflecting the dance of the waves onto the gunwale of the boat. Before posting she captions it. *Time is like the ocean; you can only hold a little in your hands.* She tags the watch manufacturer, then carefully chooses a few hashtags for maximum engagement, and pockets her phone as she hits the doorway.

"There you are." Bodhi's mom—and her boss—Robin calls from the cash register. She must have come in while Willa was sneaking around on other people's boats with a lifted watch. Willa's stomach twists. She casually slips the watch off and positions it on the display rack with the other watches and timers. "Did you take that?" Robin says, not looking up from the till. She's a tall, broad-shouldered woman with short gray hair and red-framed glasses that rest alternatively on the edge of her nose or on a silver chain around her neck.

"Yep," Willa says. "Just doing a sponsored post."

"Did it do okay?"

Willa doesn't have to look to know that it did. The sailing posts always do well, racking up thousands of likes and hundreds of followers on a regular basis. Sailing-Willa is vastly more interesting than any other iteration of herself that she's tried.

Bodhi appears from the back of the store with a head nod and a "wassup." She's windswept and smells like bug spray and sunscreen, so Willa was right about her being off kayaking in the sound. "Did you get something at the cafe?" she says after yawning.

"Yeah, but I ate half of it." Grimacing at the ache in her bruised shoulder and scraped palm and elbow, Willa hefts the rest of the boxes of new merchandise to stock the apparel section. "Sorry."

"That's cool," Bodhi says, ambiguously once again, then, "Hey, did you wipe out?"

"Oh. Yeah." Willa tries to shift the weight of the boxes to her left side. "Almost ran into some pain-in-the-ass tourist not watching where they were going."

Robin tuts. "Ooh. On your bad shoulder too. I'll get some ice."

Willa drops the boxes. Right. She'd forgotten. "Yeah, it seemed like it was finally starting to get better too." She makes a show of rubbing her right shoulder and grimacing more dramatically. Yes. Her *injured shoulder*. The one that she told everyone is preventing her from ever sailing again. That injured shoulder. The fake one.

CH. 3

It didn't start as a lie. She really did injure her shoulder right before she got the job at Porter Sails. It was stupid injury: She was at a party the night before her interview and was a little tipsy when she tripped and went down shoulder first. So at the interview, when Bodhi's other mom Jenn asked how often she sailed, Willa took a breath and shrugged, meaning to tell her that well, actually, she didn't, and that certainly disqualified her from working at a sailing store, but the movement made her hiss and wince.

"Oh, are you injured?" Jenn asked then, her soft brown eyes full of the sort of sympathy and caring and attention that Willa yearned most for back then. So she played it up, just a little.

"Yeah, I—" Willa winced and tenderly touched her shoulder for dramatic effect. "I think maybe I tore something? Like, permanently?" Well, for all she knew, she had.

Jenn frowned sympathetically. "That makes sailing difficult, I bet."

Willa had read an article about applying for a job when you aren't qualified for it and remembered that it said to not talk about one's shortcomings and instead to emphasize *transferable skills*. "That's what makes this job so perfect! I can share my love of sailing without being out on a boat!"

That was true. And if Robin and Jenn assumed that she had injured herself sailing and that she could never sail again and that all of her sailing expertise was from personal experience and not YouTube videos and secondhand knowledge, well, she hadn't outright lied. And she *does* love sailing—in theory. She also really needed a job, or her grandparents were going to kick her out, and the tiny island doesn't exactly have a wealth of jobs to choose from.

Her work mostly consists of running the cash register and answering customer questions, plus promoting the store on social media, so the experienced sailor facade is fairly easy to maintain. Today, as on most days since the weather turned, she's not even doing that. Instead, Willa scrolls Instagram and zones out, hunched over the checkout desk with her chin propped on her fist. Bodhi tries on life vests nearby.

"Does this one go with my skin tone?" It's neon yellow.

"Mm-hmm," Willa says.

Bodhi sways side-to-side, posing model-like over her shoulder as she does so. She's pretty, in an earthy-beach-bum way, with her dark blonde hair, green eyes, and freckles, but Willa lives with her and thus knows Bodhi's hygiene habits intimately and so could never find her attractive—not with the way she clips her toenails.

"With the crotch strap or without?" Bodhi says.

"With, obviously."

The door chimes, and a customer enters. Willa looks over, startles, then slides off the stool and onto the floor as if her bones suddenly turned liquid. Bodhi's face appears over the edge of the stand. "Uh…"

"It's her," Willa hisses. The dark, sharp eyes. The pointed chin, lifted haughtily. The shining raven hair and deep voice as she asks—demands—if anyone is working here. It's her. "The chick I ran into this morning."

"Oh." Bodhi disappears, then reappears. She's still wearing the neon yellow life vest. "She's hot, did you run her over on purpose?"

"No!" Willa moves to a crouching position instead of being a human puddle on the floor. "And I didn't run her over; I ran *into* her. And it was, like, at least half her fault anyway."

Bodhi's face is impassive. "Okay." She disappears again.

Willa crouches behind the counter. She listens as Bodhi helps the woman find a lightweight, waterproof fleece jacket and begins to regret her possibly dramatic fall to the floor. Where does she go from here? It's not as if they're mortal enemies on the cusp of a duel to the death at sunrise; they're just strangers who had an unfortunate run-in. But it's too late, Willa is committed to stay crouched on the floor until she leaves; it's not as if she can now jump up and yell "surprise!" as though hiding from customers is just one of the many fun perks Porter Sails offers.

Willa's foot is falling asleep, and then Bodhi's legs appear behind the register, thank god. She starts to ring the woman up, and then four more legs appear, two in medium-wash denim and two in loose linen pants. Willa looks up. "Heyyyyyy, Robin and Jenn. I'm just, um…" Willa pats the ground as if she's looking for something and doesn't finish the sentence.

"Willa, dear, are you okay?" Jenn asks.

Robin puts her hands on her hips. "I think you got more hurt than you let on when that person ran into you this morning."

Willa's eyes widen. And then the person who *ran into her* leans over the checkout desk, spots Willa crouched on the floor, and looks at her with even more judgement and contempt than she had this morning.

"Um," Willa tries to find something to say that won't out her as a—a *truth-stretcher*—to Robin and Jenn or a good-for-nothing, careless jerk to the person she was a careless jerk to. "I, uh. Lost an earring?"

* * *

WILLA LOVES THE OCEAN IN winter. There's a settled peace on the empty beach where she eats a microwaved burrito she bought from the nearby gas station. It's still cold in the middle.

In the summer, when the beach is busy and bright and hot, the ocean is joyful and full of promise, but in the winter the churning gray waves and cold abandoned beach are haunted, a cold reminder that the ocean exists for itself and not for the people who splash in its waves.

"Do you ever feel like you're wasting your time?" Willa's voice is carried on the whipping wind to where Bodhi sits cross-legged next to her on the sand drinking from a carton of chocolate milk.

"Time is an illusion," Bodhi says, off-hand, as if it's just something she's heard people say to sound deep and cynical. "Or something."

"I don't mean like, philosophically," Willa says, picking up a pinto bean that fell on her lap. "I mean, aren't we supposed to be discovering who we are right now? Trying new things? Living our best lives?" It's as if her teens were spent faking it until she figured out who she was, only she never got to the place where she *becomes* someone. Maybe she is just fucking around.

Bodhi takes a thoughtful sip of her chocolate milk. "I dunno, man. We get to be part of that every day." She nods at the waves. "We're not tied down or running the rat race. Having freedom and the ocean? Doesn't get much better than that."

"Yeah," Willa says, but remains unsettled. The reality is that Bodhi gets to be free in a way that Willa can't; she gets to coast while Willa has to tread water and gasp for every breath. She can't say any of that though, because she needs Bodhi to think they're the same, otherwise the entire bedrock of their friendship will crumble beneath the lies.

"You okay, dude? You seem off today." Bodhi, for all her unaware super-chillness, is at heart a genuinely kind person. Having her and Robin and Jenn means the world to Willa.

"Yeah, I dunno. I think the weather is getting to me." She huddles her arms around her knees order to emphasize this notion.

"I hear you. I have half a mind to sail down to the Keys just for some warmth."

Willa nods, as if that's something she's ever done, and her phone starts to vibrate with dozens of notifications coming in at once. She pulls her phone out, expecting likes and comments on the beach picture she just posted. It's a black and white shot of old pier posts leading out into the ocean. The caption reads: *We know only too well that what we are doing is nothing more than a drop in the ocean. But if the drop was not there, the ocean would be missing something.*

There are likes and comments on the post, but the flurry of activity is because she's been repeatedly tagged on something. Willa unlocks her phone, opens the app, and sits up straight. It's a sailing competition. One that's coming here. A sailing competition that's coming here that dozens of people seem to think she should participate in. She, Willa, who cannot sail but has told everyone she knows and thousands of strangers on the Internet that she can.

"Oh, crap," Willa says out loud.

CH. 4

WILLA MOVED TO PORTER ISLAND from Ohio when she was three, after her parents split. It was an ugly breakup, or so her mom said, and, since her father never bothered to come around and tell his side of the story, that's the version she believes. Young and broke and desperate for a new start, her mom came here to the vacation home her parents own, where she'd spent many happy childhood summers.

So Willa grew up swimming in the ocean, with sand on her skin and salt in her frizzy curls. When the boat regattas were in town she and her mom would pack bologna sandwiches and freshly squeezed lemonade and go to the beach to watch the sailboats skim past. "Imagine being that free," her mom would say. "Just you and the wind, the sea, and the sky."

Imagining was the closest she ever got.

Most of the kids Willa went to school with had parents who owned the construction companies that built the beautiful ocean-front homes or ran the hotels that attracted hordes of tourists or owned the restaurants and shops where said hordes dumped their money. Willa's mom worked long hours cleaning rooms at one of those fancy hotels. Willa told everyone she was the night manager.

When Willa was sixteen, her mom remarried, and, when she was seventeen, her mom and new stepdad moved to Kansas City, and Willa stayed. And then they had two kids and her mom and her mom's new husband stopped coming for visits. Since then, she has had to look out for her own self-interest more than ever, because no one else will. Maybe her choices aren't quite on the straight and narrow sometimes, but she has do what she has to do to stay afloat. And that's why it's impossible for her to escape this damn boat race.

Initially, she dismisses the idea completely. Walking back to the sail shop with Bodhi, with their clothes shedding sand and Bodhi waxing poetic about her favorite places in Key Largo, Willa types up a quick post addressing everyone who has pointed out the upcoming regatta. *I would love to do this,* she writes, over a melancholy blue background, *so badly. And I'm super stoked this comp is coming to our little island, but it looks like I missed the entry window.* A few sad-face emojis and a boat emoji and a heart emoji, and that's that, until she's clocking out and notices even more notifications, then stops cold outside the back door.

"Someone entered me," she says.

"What was that, dear?" Robin's office chair squeaks as she leans back toward the hallway.

Crap, she didn't mean to say that out loud. "Oh, nothing. Just, gosh, I really wish I could enter this race, but there's an entry fee, so."

"Oh, Bodhi mentioned that." She takes off her reading glasses and folds them thoughtfully. "You know, if you really want to do it we could certainly sponsor you. It's a major competition, lots of eyeballs on it. It would be great publicity for the shop."

"That... would be awesome," Willa says, even as she feels her withered soul exit her body. "So, so awesome."

"Of course, there is the matter of your shoulder."

Yes! Her shoulder. Oh, thank god.

"God, yeah. If only my shoulder wasn't an issue," Willa says, with a sigh and a frown and heads home, relieved that one of her lies is coming back to help instead of haunt her.

"I think it's become like a metaphor," Bodhi says later, at home.

"What?" They'd been sitting in silence, well, silence minus the thunk-thud, thud-thunk of the barstool where Bodhi sways side-to-side.

15

"Your shoulder. Ma said you really want to race again, but it's holding you back. But I was thinking, the injury itself isn't the problem. It's the *idea* of it."

Stomach sinking at how dangerously close Bodhi is to figuring her out, Willa snaps, "Pretty sure it's the actual injury, Bo."

"No, dude." Bodhi stops swaying and, uncharacteristically serious, looks at Willa. "I've gotten hurt while sailing, too, and it's scary, I get it. But if you can't get back up and push through it, you're sunk for real. I mean, didn't you say you wanted to be living your best life or something? Isn't this a chance to do that?"

What can she say? It is. Willa nods. She's trapped. She's out of excuses, unless she comes clean and tells everyone on social media and in her life that she's standing on a starboard of lies. "A boat!" It's Bodhi's turn to look alarmed at the non sequitur. "I don't have a boat. Can't race without a boat." Bodhi's sailboat isn't meant for racing, and Robin and Jenn own an old cumbersome cruiser, and all the rentals in the marina are meant for leisurely day trips around the islands, and it's not as if she can just go out and buy one.

Oh, thank god.

The next morning at work she drops a box of quick-release shackles and loses ten years of her life after someone comes up behind her and claps.

"Sorry to frighten you."

Willa thought she was alone in the store and isn't sure how she missed someone coming in. "Mr. Kelley. It's okay. Guess I was in the zone." He owns the marina next door, where he rents out the slips and rents, sells, and services boats. He's an older man, with a heavy eastern North Carolina accent and the chapped, leathery skin of someone who spends most of their time outdoors. He's nice, always lets Willa lurk around his marina for boat pictures. He encourages it, even, as long as she stumps for him.

"Heard you were in need of a boat."

Oh, no. "Mr. Kelley I couldn't possibly ask you to—"

16

He holds up a dry, pink hand; his watery blue eyes fill with deep sincerity. "It'd be my honor, truly. I've watched you scamper around on those boats. I see the way you look at 'em. How could I not let you take one out to follow your dream? I believe in you, kid. I won't take no for an answer. Honestly, it'd break my heart if you didn't use it."

How the hell is she supposed to refuse that?

That night, while staring at the ceiling instead of sleeping, Willa cycles through the many harrowing stages of letting a little white lie get well and truly out of hand. Maybe, she thinks, maybe she is good at sailing and just doesn't know it. Maybe she's even a sailing prodigy, nothing but raw, untapped talent that she's been too afraid to tap into. She has a lot of theoretical knowledge, which *has* to mean something. She can skateboard and surf a little, which is, like, basically, almost the same thing. Right? It's possible this entire thing will blow up in her face in an epically humiliating way. In fact, that's the most likely scenario. But what if it isn't? What. If.

This is insane. Willa flops onto her stomach and lets her arm dangle off the bed. She can't just hop on a boat and expect to win a sailing regatta that attracts some of the best competitors from all over the world. No, of course she can't. But if she can...

Willa flops back over. Terror and excitement and extreme misgivings war in her gut. If she can actually win it, not only can she save herself from being found out as a fraud, she could also win the ten thousand dollar prize. No more couch surfing in the summer. No more scrounging for change to buy breakfast or splitting half a burrito with Bodhi for lunch. She could buy a car. She could get a place that's really hers. She could pay off credit card debt. She could go back to school and do... something. She could do *something.*

Willa sits up in bed; excitement finally wins. She's gonna do it. She has a boat, an entry fee, people who believe in her, and the audacity to believe that she can, which is certainly the most important part. She can do this.

CH. 5

She can't do this.

On her next day off, Willa goes to the marina with pep in her step and hope in her heart and boards the sailboat that Mr. Kelley points out. It's a tidy little racer, white with sails striped in purple and orange and blue. "She ain't fancy, but she's fast," Mr. Kelley says as he watches Willa carefully climb aboard. The boat is designed to be operated by a single sailor, so it's a snug fit, even with the mainsail rolled up and the boom swung away toward starboard. The dinghy wobbles as Willa settles into it, and her stomach follows suit.

Preparing to set sail is a simple procedure. She's watched and read about it dozens of times. Just check that the lines aren't tangled, pull them onto their cleats and off their winches, watch the boom, secure the tiller, then hoist. Simple. Willa scans the lines and the sail and the boom, takes a breath and—nothing. Her hands won't move; her arms won't reach; her legs won't un-crouch. What if she ties a knot incorrectly and something gets tangled or, worse, slips free? What if she can't figure out how to direct the sails? What if she can't even make it out of the marina? What if the tiller isn't attached correctly, and she can't steer out in the open water? What if the boom isn't cleated and it swings out and knocks her into the ocean? Willa chances a look over the port side. The water looks cold; better not risk it.

"Gettin' to know her a bit?" Mr. Kelley calls. He's replacing some boards on the dock nearby, probably to keep an eye on her. Because he *believes in her*, which is just frickin' great.

"Oh. Yep." She pats the boat as if it's a dog. "She's a beauty! Maybe I'll sail away and never come back!" Willa fake-laughs, and Mr. Kelley chuckles and gives her an *oh, you* gesture. It's not a half-bad idea. Sail away and disappear, and then no one will ever find out what a big faking faker she is. She can start a new life on a new island. Or hey, maybe she'll get lucky and fall overboard. She can only sit in the boat and do nothing for so long before Mr. Kelley will get suspicious, so she mumbles an excuse about needing to get home before dark. She takes it slow on her skateboard, coasting down the streets as if spinning out the daylight hours is going to somehow help her out of this predicament.

When she was a kid, well before she ever picked up a skateboard, Willa was invited to a classmate's birthday party at a roller-skating rink over on the mainland. Overconfident in her ability to roller-skate despite never having tried it before, she strapped on a pair of heavy brown skates, hopped into the rink, and immediately bit it; she landed ass-first on the hard, shiny wood floor. The lesson should have been that learning something new requires patience and hard work and perhaps a decent helping of humility. But Willa lied, saying she hurt her ankle, and then watched the rest of the party have fun from behind a plastic wall. Full of hubris, she picked up skateboarding soon after that; she asked her grandparents to send her a skateboard for her birthday. She was just as bad at that, but she practiced riding behind a dumpster at the hotel while her mom worked. That way no one ever saw her fall.

In short: She's fucked, and there's only one thing she can do.

"Hey, Mom."

"Hi! Is everything okay?" Her mom's tone is worried, an indication that Willa should probably call more often.

"Yeah. No. I dunno." Willa sighs. "Honestly, I'm dealing with kind of a situation?" Understatement. A thud and a screech drown out her mom's response. "What? Mom?"

"Wha—" Another screech. "Hold on, Willa, okay?"

Willa sits on the bottom step of the cottage's porch stairs and listens to the faint sounds of her mom dealing with her kids. Willa knows it's not true, not really, but it seems sometimes as if her mom started over without Willa. She finally got the relationship and family and life she always wanted, and Willa is just that first messed up pancake in a batch that she started too soon, too young, before she got the hang of it and made things right.

A pack of bikes is parked next to Bodhi's bicycle, and muddy kayaks lie abandoned in the dirt driveway. Bodhi has friends over. That'll really hinder Willa's evening plan to wallow in self-pity.

"You still there, honey?" A little breathless and sounding frazzled, her mom comes back on the line. "Now, what were you saying? About a situation?"

"It's—" Willa starts, only to be interrupted again by someone crying.

"Let me put on a video for them; hold on."

"No, it's fine. Honestly, it was nothing. Just wanted to chat." Her mom starts to protest, but Willa cuts her off. "Seriously, I'm fine. I'll call tomorrow." She won't, but she hangs up on the fake promise anyway. Amelia and Atticus are little, and Willa is an adult. She had her mom all to herself for almost nineteen years. They need her more now. It's fine. She'll figure it out on her own; she usually does.

The cottage is thick with patchouli- and weed-scented smoke, and The String Cheese Incident or some other meandering, identical-sounding jam band plays from a phone dropped upside down into a glass on the coffee table. "Hey," Willa says, to the gathering of people lounging on the couch and floor and counter barstools. She knows all of them; Porter Island, for all its pristine coastal paradise reputation, is a small town at its core. Yet they're all only Willa's friends by proxy; they're Bodhi's friends who hang out with Willa because she's there.

"Wills." Bodhi scrambles up from the floor. She digs something out of her beat-up old backpack and drops it on the counter. It's a local newspaper, thin and gray, *The Porter Tribune* stamped in huge blue letters on the top. "How'd it go today? Sailing again?" Bodhi's eyes are bright; her grin is expectant and proud.

Several pairs of eyes turn to her and, as much as Willa wants to come clean and ask Bodhi for help, tell her that she's in over her head and doesn't know to do, she can't. "It... went okay."

Bodhi nods knowingly. "I'm sure you're rusty. Don't sweat it; it'll come back to you." *Right.* She taps the newspaper. "Check it out."

Willa frowns and unfolds the paper. She hasn't read a newspaper in years and, in fact, could have sworn the local paper went belly-up a while ago—or at least went digital.

"Maritime Heritage on Display This Weekend at Wooden Boat Show," Willa reads. Bodhi flips the paper over and points again. Willa scans reports about hurricane damage and a police chief retiring down to *Local Sailor Nabs Spot in Prestigious Sailing Regatta.* Willa's stomach drops.

No. No, no, no, no.

"Is that—" It's her own face; her own hazel eyes stare back at her from the front page. She feels faint.

"My moms sent it in!" Bodhi's smile turns radiant. "Sweet, right?"

"You're famous!" Bodhi's good friend Hunter—always around, always annoying—says from the barstool next to her. She's either joking or really stoned; it's hard to say. *Famous* is stretch, but the whole town knowing about this is not good at all. "Better hope you aren't rusty for too long," Hunter says. "I mean, what if you screwed up in front of the whole town with *everyone* watching. That would be so embarrassing, oh, my god."

Willa slams the paper down. "Do you think, Hunter? Do you think it would be embarrassing? Do you think maybe I'm already under a lot of pressure, and that isn't *fucking helping, Hunter.*" She only realizes how loud she was yelling when the room goes totally silent, not counting the aimless mandolin solo coming from a glass.

"Whoa, dude."

*   *   *

Bodhi comes into Willa's room after everyone is gone. It's past midnight, but Willa is cross-legged on her bed. The only slight illumination is the blue light of her phone.

"Want a hot dog?"

Willa's stomach growls; she's been shut in her room for hours now, too humiliated and ashamed to come out and scrounge for food. She reaches for the bag. "Thanks." She's known Bodhi long enough to be aware that she holds nothing against anyone, but Willa appreciates the peace offering all the same.

"You don't have to do it, you know. The comp."

"I know." Willa unwraps a hot dog; the rustling seems overloud in the quiet cottage. Bodhi doesn't compete. She says she doesn't have the disposition for it, and that's probably true. If she explained everything, Bodhi would understand. She would forgive Willa; she'd probably even take pity on her and teach her how to sail. The thought makes Willa's bite of hot dog hard to swallow. She doesn't want Bodhi's pity and she doesn't want to disappoint Robin and Jenn or even Mr. Kelley. She can't ruin her online reputation and lose all her hard-won followers and she doesn't want her mom to think she can't handle her own life like an adult. She doesn't want to be a loser just *fucking around* doing nothing and she doesn't want to be the laughingstock of the whole town. "But I am." Going to do the competition come hell or high water, that is.

Bodhi nods and pushes off the doorjamb. "Okay. Well, don't be afraid to ask for help if you need it. People usually train for these things, you know."

Train. *Train.* That's it. That's the key. Willa drops her uneaten chunk of hot dog on the blanket and drags her ancient laptop from underneath her bed. Training. Of course!

CH. *6*

WILLA'S QUEST FOR A TRAINER goes well into the early morning. She spends hours huddled under a blanket with food debris surrounding her and her old laptop valiantly chugging along. She searches for local sailing coaches and finds only collegiate teams and private yacht club offerings and, since she isn't in college and has a training budget of nothing, those won't quite work. She tries local sailing schools on some nearby islands and the mainland, but they only offer beginner lessons for recreational sailing, nothing for racing. Hoping for some type of lead somewhere, Willa moves on to researching the race itself.

HIGH SEAS, the website blares, *single-handed ocean racing at its most challenging. Only for the most courageous of skippers, High Seas brings prestige and respect for those who endeavor to drive themselves and their boat to the limit.*

"Seems dramatic," Willa mumbles, scooping up a brownie crumb. She scans videos and pictures of past races and reads through the bios of past winners. The sun begins to press against her windows; a few birds tentatively chirp their morning song. Soon the ferry will lumber from its port, and, if she wants to get any sleep at all, she'll need to finish this Internet spiral another day. But then, for the first time since she started down this snowballing path of increasingly bad ideas, Willa has a stroke of luck: a two-year-old interview with a past winner, Lane Cordova, discussing her imminent retirement from sailing.

"Overall I'm proud of what I've done," Lane Cordova, four-time High Seas champion says in the blurb. "I know I've left a legacy of achievement, and that's a great note to end on." There's a picture of her in action, covered from head to toe in yellow rain gear, wind at her back, standing confidently at the helm, yellow-hooded face obscured, and facing determinedly out at the stormy sea. Lane Cordova, the caption says, will join her family's real estate business on Porter Island, North Carolina.

Willa flings the blanket from her shoulders and grins. "Lane Cordova, I could kiss you!"

Blue Sky Realty is in a single-story, hut-like building with blue clapboard siding and white Bahama shutters pushed open and away from the large windows. It's across the street and down a ways from the Sand Dollar Cafe, and Willa has probably skated past it thousands of times without thinking much about the building at all. Today, she tucks her board under her arm, winds up the walkway decorated with shells and non-native palm fronds, and walks under a sea-glass wind chime into the front lobby. Pale wood floors, a high wooden desk, and a collection of wicker chairs greet her inside.

"Hello, and how may I help you today?" The receptionist's tone is friendly in a completely disingenuous way.

"I'm looking for, um." This seemed like a great idea after three hours of sleep and a Red Bull, but under the scrutiny of the red-lipsticked and thick-mascaraed receptionist, Willa isn't sure what she thought would really happen. "Lane… Cordova?"

The receptionist smiles, over-widely. "Ms. Cordova is out at a showing presently, but she should be back within the hour if you'd like to wait." She tilts her head. "Or I'm happy to take a message."

"I'll wait." Willa sits in a chair that creaks and cracks beneath her and leans her board against the side. The lobby is painted faint green and decorated with beach-themed black and white photos. One wall has a row of various accolades, plaques, and glass trophies announcing awards of distinction for realtors all with the last name Cordova, but none of them Lane. Willa is seized with momentary panic that maybe Lane Cordova didn't come here to work at her family's business at all. But the receptionist certainly would have cheerfully sent her on her way if that was true. Is this what Lane Cordova left a distinguished sailing career behind for? To not make it onto her own family's wall of fame?

Willa stands to get a closer look, and then the front door opens. Someone bustles in, someone in gray dress slacks, black heels, a gray blazer, and a white button-down. Shoulders high, back straight, she walks with confidence and no-nonsense poise. Willa stands, stomach sinking as she takes in the chin-length black hair, the thick eyebrows drawn down in a scowl, and that familiar pointed chin, lifted high to better look down her nose at everyone.

"You," Willa mutters.

The woman barely spares her a contemptuous glance before striding down a hallway; the slam of a door follows moments after. Willa gapes; dawning realization turns to horror as she considers the possibility that— That she— She can't possibly be—

"Ms. Cordova will see you now."

Willa should walk out the door and never come back. That would be the smart thing to do, the reasonable thing. She could find someone else to train her. Or, perhaps, she could walk out the door, keep walking, take the ferry to the mainland, change her name, and disappear from general society and then this will all go away forever. Willa has, unfortunately, never been prone to reasonableness. She blows out a breath and marches herself down the hallway until she reaches a glass door to an office where Lane Cordova sits behind a shiny black desk and scowls at a computer. Willa knocks and enters.

"Come to spill something else on me?"

Willa raises her empty hands.

Lane grunts. "Sit." She gestures at an upholstered chair across from her desk. "Unless you'd prefer the floor."

She planned it all out somewhere around three a.m. She would come to Lane Cordova with the story that Willa is a gifted sailor who has simply had a run of bad luck and a bad shoulder and that she wants to prove to the world she's still got it. And Lane, a former champion herself—one of only two women to ever win High Seas—would take pity on Willa's plight and jump at the chance to help her. Willa would learn to race from the best and thus not completely humiliate herself during the competition and after that she can get back to her regular low-key, low-stress life and never tell another lie again. In the wee hours of the morning while chugging an energy drink, this seemed like a fail-proof plan—a genius one, even. But sitting across from Lane's stormy expression and tightly crossed arms, Willa is pretty sure she can't count on Lane's empathy.

"I, uh, am looking to buy a house."

One of Lane's dark, sculpted eyebrows lifts. "Is that so."

"Yes." Willa nods and *mm-hmms.* "Yep."

Lane studies her for a long, tense moment. Never in her life has Willa felt so much like a fish flayed open, her most hidden and tender parts yanked out and exposed to the bright light of day. Willa squirms in the armless armchair.

"Well then." Her deep, rough-edged voice and humorless tone still Willa's nervous fidgeting. "Let's find you a house."

CH. 7

JUST IN CASE SHE WASN'T in deep enough, Willa tells Lane Cordova that she's been approved for a four-hundred thousand dollar loan, a number she pulled entirely out of thin air, and that she's looking for a home with "a view" because it seemed like something people looking for a home would say. She then snaps a picture of the house Lane takes her to and posts it with a caption reading, "Time to give up the beach cottage? LMK in the comments!"

With arms crossed and eyes narrowed, Lane waits outside her immaculately maintained SUV. "Would you like to see the inside or would you prefer to livestream a tour of the porch?"

If Lane is always this brusque and impatient, Willa can see why she doesn't have her name on any of those fancy plaques. "Yep! I like what I see so far!" That, at least, is true. Where her grandparents' cottage is snug and cozy and simple in design, the house is open and spacious with a wraparound porch, high ceilings, and huge windows. From the front windows in the huge living room, Willa can see the sound. She does, in fact, livestream the tour.

"It's three beds, two-and-a-half baths, and the lot is just under a quarter-acre. It's listed at five ninety-nine. Now I know you said four, but you aren't going to find much for that. As a matter of fact, this one is not going to last, so, if you like it, I'd advise putting in an offer today." Lane's jaw works, and her chin lifts.

"That makes sense," Willa replies easily. She turns the camera on herself. "Things are getting real y'all! Hey, can I see the upstairs?"

After touring three large, light-infused bedrooms, Lane shows her a recently remodeled master bath with double sinks, a separate shower stall done in stonework, and a garden tub that Willa climbs into. Her followers are really responding to this house; Willa is convinced she could sell the place herself within minutes. "I can see myself being happy here," Willa says, ending the successful stream and stretching out in the tub. She should pretend to look at real estate more often. Lane sighs and takes her down the polished wooden staircase. Willa decides to investigate the kitchen more thoroughly; she opens and closes the fridge, counts cabinets and drawers, then muses that it's too bad that the range is electric instead of gas.

"Okay, I know you aren't really buying this house. Or any house." Lane says suddenly, as if she couldn't hold it in any longer. "What is this? A prank? A, a YouTube challenge? Are you punking me? Am I on *Punked*?"

Willa blinks, hands still on the oven handle, unsure of the best way to respond. Deflection? Defensiveness? She goes with confusion. "What's *Punked*?"

"God, are you—" Lane squeezes the bridge of her nose. "Are you even a legal adult?"

"I'm twenty-two," Willa says, defensive, though she's well aware that her round eyes, soft cheeks, and button nose make her look like a middle schooler.

"Twenty-two," Lane mutters, rubbing between her eyes as if she's fighting off a headache. "And are you actually interested in buying a house? Honestly."

Willa is ready to defend herself. "Of course I am," she should say. "Why else would I be looking at houses with you? To slowly gain your trust and then work in casual references to sailing until I've convinced you to train me? How could you imply such a thing?" But something in Lane's expression stops her cold. What Willa thought was stuck-up judgment now looks more like insecurity and defensiveness. And that is something Willa can relate to.

"No." Willa turns away from the oven and shoves her hands in the pockets of her torn jeans. "I'm not."

"Then why," Lane says, voice and expression hardening. "Are you *wasting my time?*"

Willa stares at her feet. Every time she's around this woman she's knocked off balance, literally and figuratively. She doesn't know where to go from here, how to make this right, other than with the truth. For once.

"Okay." She releases a long breath. "I was entered into High Seas because everyone thinks I'm this great sailor with an old injury keeping me from competing, but that's a lie. I don't know how to sail at all, not really. And I was hoping you would train me, since you won it, and then maybe I won't look like a total idiot and let down everyone I know." Willa winces; saying it out loud makes it all seem so much worse.

Lane stares, absorbing this information. Willa notices for the first time how uncomfortable Lane is in her business-casual realtor look, how she's constantly pulling on the stiff collar of her shirt and shifting her weight off her high-heeled feet. It doesn't even fit right, the suit; it's too long at the hem and too boxy in the shoulders, like when Willa had to ditch her board shorts and T-shirts to go to Ohio for Thanksgiving with her grandparents. She'd let her mom pick out the dress because she was going to hate it no matter what and just had to tolerate it for the day. Taking the dress off at night was more than shedding uncomfortable clothes; it was as if she was taking off an entire persona.

"And why would I help you?" Lane finally says.

Willa attempts a winning grin. "Sisterhood?" Lane rolls her eyes. Willa has to think fast; Lane is her last hope. Maybe they didn't get off to the *best* start, and if Willa had known she was a local real estate agent instead of an annoying tourist maybe she would have tried to mend fences sooner, especially because Lane seems to be struggling compared to the rest of her family. *That's it.* "I can help you," Willa says.

"I don't want to learn how to skateboard," Lane says sarcastically. "But thanks."

"You can sponsor me. It's a televised competition, and I'll share it all on social media. That's a lot of eyeballs on your real estate business. On you."

Lane doesn't immediately reject the idea, which means Willa might have a chance.

"I don't think so..."

"I have five hundred thousand Instagram followers."

"I don't—" Lane's head tilts. "Five hundred thousand?"

"Yep." Willa lifts to her toes. "And that's just Instagram."

Skepticism crosses Lane's face. "High Seas is no joke. What if you immediately capsize and die? That doesn't seem like great PR for me."

Willa shrugs, unruffled by the implication of imminent doom. "Everyone will be talking about it either way."

Lane's eyes narrow, and Willa's mind spins desperately for a way to convince Lane to help her. Suddenly, she has a flash of an idea, recalling the wall of plaques at the real estate office—none of which were engraved with Lane's name. Lane, who was world champion at sea but apparently not so much on land.

"Your family's office has so many awards. Who is Charles Junior? Your brother?" Willa gives a low whistle. "How many does he have would you say?"

Lane's face hardens; her jaw flexes and her nose flares. Willa is certain she's hit the wrong button, that Lane is going to send her out on her ass, but then Lane sighs. Her shoulders drop. She directs an unfocused gaze out of the oversized living room windows. There's a long, heavy pause and then, "You know what? Okay. Yeah. Why the hell not."

Willa shouts in excitement, but Lane holds up a finger. "Only enough so that you don't kill yourself before you even get the anchor up. A few times out. That's it. I make no promises that you will finish the race, let alone win it."

"Yes, okay. Understood." Willa bounces with the effort of not squealing with joy. Lane Cordova *is* the answer to her prayers. She knew it. And she could still, maybe, kinda, sorta, kiss her for it. Maybe.

CH. 8

WILLA DOESN'T HEAR FROM LANE right away. Weeks pass, and nothing. Winter rolls in, turning the island still and cold. The shop is dead. The beaches are empty. Bodhi spends most of her time burrowed in her bed, hibernating like a freckled blonde bear, and Willa spends most of her time waiting: waiting for her phone to ring or a text to come, waiting for her endless shifts at the sail shop to be over, waiting for likes and comments, waiting for sleep, waiting for morning. On the coldest day of the season so far, she finally gets a text from Lane, asking for her address and saying she'll be over in twenty minutes.

Maybe I'm busy, Willa texts back. Presumptuous.

Are you? Lane sends in reply. Willa has spent the last twenty minutes on the couch trying get marshmallows to land on top of one of the slowly spinning fan blades above her. She's been waiting for Lane to get back to her for ages and had nearly given up. But still. Presumptuous.

I can be available in twenty, Willa replies.

As she gets ready to go, Bodhi emerges, bleary-eyed and wearing only a T-shirt and underwear with a blanket loosely wrapped around her. Her bed-head manages to look casually disheveled, like a celebrity dressed down to go to the grocery store, unlike the frizz-fest that Willa contends with every morning.

"Can I use your foul weather gear?" Willa asks as Bodhi rummages through the once-again-sparse pantry and fridge. The race takes place in the spring, which should mean that Willa won't have to hustle for sponsored posts to grift for her own insulated and waterproof pants, coat, gloves, boots, and hat.

"Yeah. Training today?" Willa nods. "Awesome," Bodhi says. "Cold as hell, dude, but awesome."

Willa goes into Bodhi's room to bundle up while Bodhi calls someone about meeting for breakfast and then fishing. Willa is pretty sure Bodhi is supposed to work today, but that's Robin and Jenn's problem for now. Well, it is every day, really, but today it is not *also* Willa's problem. Willa finds the coat and pants in the back of the second bedroom's closet; they're both bright blue and thick, made of slippery vinyl fabric. She has to jump to reach the hat and gloves and boots on the top shelf and curses when the rubber boots clatter down onto the hardwood floor. Someone in the bed groans and rolls over, still asleep.

"Why didn't you tell me you had company?" Willa hisses after closing the door behind her. Don't they have a system for this? Sock on the doorknob? A head's up of some sort?

Bodhi shrugs. She's plunked down cross-legged on the couch, scooping up handfuls of marshmallows and shoving them into her mouth. "It's just Hunter."

Willa steps into the pants and pulls the straps over her shoulders, then shrugs on the jacket. "Hunter? Are you guys…?" Last she knew, Bodhi and Hunter were just friends, though, given the lack of options on the island, sometimes "just friends" turns into something else. It's unfortunate if so, because Hunter hangs around them too much as it is.

"It's whatever." Bodhi's response is garbled by a mouthful of marshmallows.

"Okay then," Willa says, as if Bodhi's answer means anything. She's pulling on the high, stiff boots when the doorbell rings. "Got it." Willa limps over, one boot partly on, opens the door to Lane, and says, with more than little irritation that she's early, "Gimme a sec."

Lane steps inside and sweeps a long, assessing gaze around the living room and kitchen. Willa finishes gearing up, glad that she was bored enough this morning to clean, though Lane clearly thinks so little of her that Willa isn't sure she could sink much lower, even with a filthy house.

"You have foul weather gear? I thought—" Bundled up in her own gear, Lane stops and glances at Bodhi. "I thought you... *quit* a while ago."

Thankful for Lane's decision to lean into Willa's lie, she decides to be more polite. "It's Bodhi's. Would you like something to drink? Water?" And on her way to the kitchen, she nods toward the couch. "This is my roommate Bodhi. Bodhi, Lane."

"Hey," Bodhi says, then holds up the bag of marshmallows in offering.

"I'm— I'm good. And I'm good on water too. We should really get going."

"Okay. I'll just get water for myself." Willa checks the cup cabinet, the dishwasher, the cabinet with a disorganized and random collection of plastic storage containers. "Bo, have you seen my water bottle?"

Bodhi stands to help, and, as she does, the blanket wrapped around her slips from her shoulders, revealing just how little she's wearing. Lane snaps her eyes to the ceiling, crosses her arms tightly across her chest, and yells, voice strained, "I have water, can we *go*."

"Okay, god. Sorry." Willa grabs her keys and phone and tugs a knit wool hat onto her head; her curls stick out like tufts of clown hair from the sides. "Let's go." Lane discovering Willa lived in a dirty, unkempt house would have been better, it turns out, than learning that she lives with a weird half-naked slacker who eats fistfuls of marshmallows for breakfast.

Lane drives them to the other side of the island, the sound-side, the southern tip of which is mostly a protected nature preserve, and then to an area where large, beautiful homes sit tucked back in the woods, facing away from the sound, all with their own private docks and slips with jet skis and multiple boats parked like a show-and-tell of wealth. Lane turns onto a narrow dirt road and drives up to a stately brick house hidden demurely behind two massive magnolia trees.

"You live here?" Willa is unable to keep the awe out of her voice.

"My parents live here. But this is where my boat is docked." Lane turns off the car and pauses with her hands on the keys. "Your roommate. She's…" Lane seems unable to decide how she wants to finish that sentence.

A weirdo? Willa guesses. "She's like, a free spirit. I dunno. It's annoying sometimes; there is such a thing as too easy-going, you know? But it's a good energy to be around." Willa unbuckles, and Lane does the same. "Bodhi's good people."

Lane nods, though her expression seems to indicate she's unsatisfied with that answer. "And she sails?"

"Oh. Yeah," Willa says, catching on now. "But not competitively. And she doesn't know, you know, that I can't."

"Right." Lane gets out of the car and walks at her purposeful pace toward the house, and Willa scrambles to catch up. They walk behind the house, past a double garage, through woods, then across the wetlands, where the line of trees gives way to shrubs, which give way to swishing sea grass and thick mud. They walk single file down a dock, and beneath them small crabs scuttle away from the thump of their footsteps. As the dock leads them over shallow water, small schools of fish dart around the wooden posts. The wind slices across the water and hits like ice on the bits of skin that Willa's gear isn't covering. Three boats are moored down a floating slip: a large daysailer, a sleek motorboat designed for water sports, and a tidy little RS Elite keelboat.

"You know, I do have a boat," Willa points out. It may be a borrowed one that is nowhere near as nice as Lane's, but still.

Lane shakes her head. "It'll be faster to show you on mine." Of course. Willa wouldn't expect Lane to spend any more time with her than is absolutely necessary. "Come on." Lane climbs into the boat with practiced ease and waits expectantly. The wind rocks the boat up and down and side to side. Up close it looks so small and insubstantial, and the ocean so rough and powerful. Willa shivers and not because of the cold. She steps forward.

CH. 9

As WILLA LOWERS HERSELF INTO the boat, the wind feels even colder, as sharp as thorns whipping against her, blowing her hair into her face. She shoves all of her hair under her hat, then shivers as the wind licks across her newly exposed neck. The boat bobs and sways as she and Lane check the rudder and lines, then hoist the mainsail, which rattles and rocks the boat back and forth with each gust. It seems foreboding: a warning that this a really bad idea. But Willa does as she's told because she trusts that Lane knows what she's doing; she has to.

This is it, the moment that she finally becomes the person she's been pretending to be. She should be excited. She should be relieved. But instead she can't stop trembling so hard that her teeth chatter and her voice shakes and her legs repeatedly threaten to go out from under her.

Lane barks instructions and scowls, a lot, and, when Willa does something wrong, she snatches the ropes and hooks from her gloved hands. "The topping lift is too loose, we need to watch out for the boom in this wind. Tighten it."

"Say please," Willa replies to Lane's yelled command, then nearly falls into her lap when the boom yanks her forward.

"*Carefully.*" Lane uses her foot to push Willa upright. "Jesus."

Willa sets her jaw and fumes; it's been nothing but yelling and eye rolling and cursing at Willa's incompetence. How is she supposed to know what to do? Isn't that why they're here? And it's freezing cold; the bitter wind fills her eyes with tears and makes her fingers ache even through the gloves. It's almost as if Lane intentionally picked the most miserable day to do this, as if she wants Willa to suffer.

"Not like that," Lane barks, again, when Willa does something wrong.

Willa spins around, body aching, tears in her eyes from the wind and from frustration. "I'm trying my best!"

"Well, your best isn't good enough," Lane yells back.

Willa spins back around, yanks the line from its winch in order to re-cleat it, *tighter*, but due to the combination of her anger at Lane, her frozen fingers and watery eyes, and the ominous, angry wind, the line slips free from her grasp. Lane reacts fast, instinctively diving for the heavy wood beam that makes up the boom, which is swinging back toward Willa. But Lane can't stop the strong forward momentum, and Willa can't get out of the way fast enough; the boom hits her in the gut and sends her falling backward, arms helplessly flailing at her sides as she goes airborne.

The water is so cold it punches the breath out of her.

And then she slips under and can't take a breath in.

Is she dead? Would she be wondering that, if she was? No. Then no, not dead. Not yet. She's disoriented. Everything is water, gray and opaque. She can't tell which way the surface is, can't find the sun or sky through the endless gray around her. She's shocked by the cold. Her brain is slow to fire off synapses; her limbs are even slower to respond when she does. *Swim,* she thinks. *Move.* Her lungs ache, desperate for a breath. She can't last much longer. Blackness spins in front of her eyes.

And then she's tugged, up, up, like a fish on a hook, and deposited on the boat deck, sputtering and gasping for air.

Lane stands over her, eyes wide and wild and hand still twisted in the collar of Willa's jacket. "Seriously? You're just gonna *drown*?" As if Willa did it on purpose, just to annoy her. Still heaving lungfuls of air and violently shivering, Willa can't do more than blink up at Lane.

Lane shakes her head, then pulls Willa up by the scruff of her neck. "Come on."

Willa shuffles along, leaving a trail of freezing water, shivering and struggling to follow Lane to the house. Lane retrieves a key from her car and takes Willa inside through a back utility room, then tells her to wait in a downstairs guest bathroom. It's bigger and nicer by far than the bathroom Willa shares with Bodhi and blissfully warm. Willa stands under a vent, face upturned, letting the gentle heat wash over her. The water-resistant foul weather gear more or less did its job; only her head and hands got truly soaked. She takes off the hat and gloves and plops them, sopping and heavy, on the marble-topped counter. Her feet are wet but not waterlogged, just damp inside of her boots. Cold water seeped in through the open collar at her neck and down her chest and back and made a damp line across her shoulders and down her chest. She drops the coat on the floor. The joggers she's wearing under the waterproof overalls are wet at the waist and ankle, bands of cold damp against her skin.

"Here." Lane returns with a stack of clothes, thrusting them out to Willa as if they're playing a game of hot potato.

"It's not that bad." Willa turns away. "Can I just use a towel—"

"Not those!" Willa pauses at Lane's outburst, stopping before she can grab one of the fluffy, pristinely white towels from a towel rack. "Those are decorative. Hold on."

Decorative. Willa eyes the towels which look like the big bath towels she uses at home, only newer and much more plush. Why have towels no one uses? They have towels in the cottage set aside for summer guests, but people *use* them. What kind of guest are they expecting? A surgeon ready to scrub in, right here in this sterile bathroom? Lane returns with a dark green towel that doesn't look much different from the forbidden white ones, but Willa takes it and dries her face and hair, which forms into tufts of frizz.

"You should still change," Lane says, still giving orders. Willa should find that irritating, but now that she's thawing out a bit it's starting to dawn on her that Lane sort of saved her life.

"Okay, I will." She tucks the towel against her chest. "Um, thanks. For. Ya know."

Lane dips her chin and walks backward out of the bathroom, closing the door behind her. When Willa emerges a few minutes later, she's dressed in a pink velour track suit that says "juicy" on the butt, paired with thick wool men's socks, and Lane is nowhere to be seen. Willa pads through a formal living room that's outfitted with furniture made of heavy wood and shining leather and gives off the same untouched air as the forbidden towels. She passes an office and a dining room filled with more polished wood and glossy leather, then walks into a den that is also outfitted with expensive-looking new furniture but that at least looks as if humans inhabited it sometime in the past decade. There's a stone fireplace with a stone mantel. There are paintings on the walls but no pictures, nothing personal, nothing to indicate anyone lives here at all. It's so strange.

"Willa?" She follows the sound of Lane's voice into a kitchen with gleaming appliances and more marble countertops. "Did you get lost?"

Willa casts a glance back at the den. "Yeah, a little."

Lane gives her an assessing look, then says, "Uh. Sorry about the outfit. Had to grab something my Mom wouldn't miss."

"Oh." Willa looks down at the flared-leg pink pants. She was so happy to be warm she barely gave the clothes a second glance. "Yeah, it's pretty terrible," she says, then winces at how ungrateful she sounds. Willa is strictly a board shorts, joggers, hoodies, and T-shirts over a bathing suit kind of person, but Lane could have just let her go home wet and cold.

To her shock, Lane gives her a kind look and sets a cup of steaming coffee on the counter. "I don't know, you're kind of pulling it off." She hands Willa a mug and stands close enough to be disconcerting. "Drink some. I don't want you to get hypothermia."

"I— I'm fine." Willa says, but wraps her hands around the warm mug anyway. She's wary of Lane's nice act. Is she getting Willa comfortable before she unleashes an angry lecture about how badly Willa screwed up and if she would just *listen*—

Catching Willa off-guard, Lane apologizes. "Uh. Some of my inner demons came out there. Those are supposed to stay buried, so that's unfortunate." She laughs, but it's tight and sharp, cold like the ocean water still clinging to Willa's hair.

"That's— I—" Scowl gone, face lit by the huge picture window in the kitchen, Lane is beautiful. Her chin is dipped, her lashes are dark against her cheeks, and her lips are softly downturned. "It's okay," Willa says, voice shaky—from the water, she thinks.

"Though, in my defense, you're really bad at it."

Willa's eyes narrow, sympathy evaporating. "Right. Okay."

"I mean, way worse than I thought and that was already a *very* low bar."

"Maybe I need a different instructor then," Willa snaps, reacting instead of thinking.

Lane nods. "You're right. I don't know if I'm the best person for this, Willa."

"Oh," Willa says. She tries to backtrack, to tell Lane that they can just try again because she really is Willa's last and only hope, but Lane catches her off-guard once more, reaching out to Willa's face and stopping with her fingertips a breath away from Willa's mouth. For the second time today, Willa freezes.

"Your lips are blue." Lane moves her hand away.

CH. *10*

WILLA HASN'T BEEN ABLE TO get warm for days. It doesn't matter how many blankets or layers she puts on, she shivers, and her fingers are like ice, and her nose is numb with cold, as if the freezing ocean water has seeped into her bones. She can't stop thinking about the moment she hit the water; her lungs seize at the memory. And she can't stop thinking about Lane and the strange moment of vulnerability in the Cordova's home.

"Maybe she just felt bad you almost died," Bodhi says, after Willa can't stop herself from musing about it out loud, again. "And, like, doesn't want you to actually die."

She gave Bodhi an abridged version of the overboard incident, blaming Lane's impatience and poor instructions instead of Willa's lack of skill and focus. And, though she was embarrassed at first and felt bad for Lane as well, the more Willa tells the story the more she seems to convince herself that she really wasn't at fault at all and that Lane just wanted to shirk any responsibility for what happened, again. "No, that can't be it."

Bodhi raises her eyebrows and turns back to the table display they've been working on. As if sensing Willa's bone-deep chill—or, more likely, because of the store's flagging winter sales—Jenn and Robin decided to put out the summer inventory early. Willa and Bodhi have been stocking the floor displays with bikinis and swim trunks and wide straw hats as well as packing up thick wetsuits and wool gloves and heavy hooded jackets.

"Maybe it is though. It's not like you really know her."

Willa considers this, straightening a row of bright red bathing suits made with just enough material to be this side of indecent, that are really only good for lounging on a deck in the sun. She *doesn't* really know Lane. In fact, every time Willa thinks she has her figured out, Lane throws her off: She's sharp-edged yet vulnerable, a local who acts like a tourist, a real estate agent who doesn't seem to sell any homes, a self-centered jerk who saves her life, someone who hates Willa but looks at her as if she wishes she didn't. A sailor who no longer sails.

After Willa left the Cordova's house—in her own clothes still humid from the dryer—she and Lane said goodbye as though that was that. The sailing lesson was a bust, and Willa was on her own to sink or swim, and they both silently acknowledged that she was doomed to sink. But if Willa is missing something, some piece of the puzzle that is the real Lane, then she can figure out a way to keep the lessons going. After all, Willa is well-versed in the ways of someone who is hiding their true self.

"You're right, Bo. I should figure her out. Follow her around, observe her from afar. Find out what her deal is without her knowing!" Willa slaps a sunhat onto the table in triumph.

Bodhi's head tips back and forth like a confused Labrador. "That's— No, that's not what I meant at all—"

"It's genius. After my shift is done, I'll go wait outside of her office."

Lane Cordova—mystery, puzzle, enigma—prepare to be solved.

*   *   *

IT'S DIFFICULT TO BE INCOGNITO with only a skateboard to hide behind, but Willa discovers after some trial and error that she can see Lane's polished SUV parked beside the real estate office from a back window in The Sand Dollar. Willa orders a peppermint hot chocolate, sits at a two-top with the chair positioned just right, and waits. She takes some artsy coffee-shop photos and posts the best ones, scrolls and likes and answers some replies. The sun sets, and the stars wink on; the windows in the real estate office turn dark, and the cars pull away from the lot. But not Lane's. Soon it's the only car in the dark parking lot across the street, and Willa worries that Lane left with someone else and she missed her. The inappropriate foolishness of this mission settles uncomfortably in her gut. What is she doing?

Finally, the headlights of the SUV snap on and beam across the cracked city road, seeming to lock right onto Willa. Willa shades her eyes and takes it as a sign. She can't follow a car on her board, of course, but she knows this island, which streets go where and why someone would take them. If Lane turns right and stays on Main, then she's heading up toward the nature preserve and the neighborhood where her parents' house sits. Left and then another quick left would mean she's running errands: She pays a water bill at city hall, stops at the small library, picks up something at the small family-owned hardware store. Left and a quick right would take her to the ferry. Right and then another right would bring Lane into the working class neighborhood where Willa lives, maybe to visit someone, maybe to visit a special someone. Willa frowns at the thought.

She watches from the sidewalk as the headlights bounce and swoop when Lane pulls out of the lot, then they flood the street as she turns right and heads straight, to the bars and restaurants and fancy resort hotels. Willa drops her board to the pavement and follows. She planned to do some detective work, carefully scanning the lots of each restaurant and bar or even the hotels to finally discover Lane's car. But Willa's first guess is the right one, and she finds Lane's SUV right by the road at The Oyster Bar, only pulled three quarters of the way into the space, as if neither it nor Lane really want to be there and hope to escape as soon as possible.

Willa stashes her board by the back door and debates what to do. She could wait, assuming that Lane just popped into the restaurant for dinner or a drink. She could creep along the windows outside, hoping to catch a glimpse of Lane, or she could just go inside and blend in instead of lurking at the windows like a creepy peeping Tom.

How goes the stakeout? Bodhi texts after Willa has settled into a corner booth with a lemonade and is staring at the back of Lane's dark head several tables down. *Boring,* Willa answers. Lane does seem to have stopped for a drink; she scrolls her phone and sips a glass of red wine at a table by herself. Willa isn't sure what she expected to find in order to justify her distrust. Did she suspect that Lane kicks puppies in her spare time or that she retires to an underground lair in the evenings, perhaps sleeping in a coffin or upside down like a bat?

Lane puts her phone down and glances at the door. She sips her wine and traces the rim of the glass with her finger. When a waiter comes by, she shakes her head. She looks at her phone, then sets it back down. Willa can't see her face, but her head is bowed and her body is drawn tight. It dawns on Willa slowly; the awfulness pushes up like a wave lapping the shore. Lane is here for a date and she's been stood up.

Willa doesn't know why and she knows she shouldn't care—Lane was probably rude and short and sharp with whomever she was supposed to meet here just as she is with Willa all the time—most of the time. Probably because she was told her whole life that nothing she does is good enough and so she's built a personality of barbed wire to protect herself, and Willa didn't have to follow her here to realize that. Willa stands from her table and walks over to Lane's. Lane will certainly tell her to get lost or silently judge her with those dark, lovely eyes. She may even figure out that Willa followed her to The Oyster Bar because somehow she sees through Willa's veneer of bullshit. This is Willa's worst idea yet. She goes anyway. She came here to find who Lane really is, but it turns out that she's already started to figure it out.

"Mind if I join you?"

CH. *11*

WILLA DOESN'T GIVE LANE a chance to answer. She sits down and immediately launches into inane chatter. She rambles on about the weather, how The Oyster bar isn't too crowded but not too empty, and how she read an article recently about a strange sudden rise in meat allergies. If she stops talking, Willa reasons, then Lane will ask her what she's doing here, and Willa doesn't have a convincing lie ready, not one Lane will believe.

"It's not just a matter of going vegan, either. Like, animal products are in medications, in vaccinations. Just smelling it cooking is enough to—"

"Willa." Lane finally cuts her off. Willa braces herself. But instead of demanding to know what the hell Willa is doing, Lane looks around the restaurant miserably then drops her head in her hands. "You know." She groans. "This is so humiliating."

"Hey, no. Everyone gets stood up, it's fine."

Lane lifts her head enough to level a look at Willa. "Have you?"

"Sure!" Willa says, too fast. Lane's eyes narrow. "I mean. Like, *technically* not—"

Lane groans again.

Willa sits quietly, unsure how to proceed. Lane is older than her, so what dating wisdom could Willa possibly impart? And yet, Lane showed up for a date directly from work, dressed in her usual ill-fitting pants suit uniform. She's nice looking without needing to try very hard, but that's the thing. She doesn't look as though she invested very much in this date. It's the same way Lane seems to approach selling houses. Her heart clearly isn't in it, but she's going through the motions anyway.

The waiter circles the table again, and Willa is just about to suggest they order something to eat when Lane thrusts her phone into Willa's face in an accusatory sort of way and demands, "Is this what people do now? Is this ghosting? Was I ghosted?"

Willa leans back to see what Lane is talking about. On her phone screen is a string of increasingly demanding messages from Lane to someone who didn't answer. "That's a lot of caps lock," Willa mutters, only to get a glare from Lane. "Look, it happens. Just forget them and move on."

Lane shakes her head, grabs her purse from the back of her chair, and takes out her wallet. "No. This was a terrible idea. I don't know how to do this." Willa watches her flag down the waiter and set a card down, and, despite her words and the obvious anger in the set of her jaw and knit of her brows, her hand shakes. Her eyes are sad.

"You don't know how to... date?" Willa's question is met with stony silence. She must have fifteen years of life experience on Willa; certainly she didn't spend it all out on a boat. Right? Lane groans again, covers her face, and makes a high hiccupping noise. *Oh, god, is she crying?* Willa looks around, as if a waiter or someone enjoying their meal nearby can help save her from this awkward situation. Should Willa comfort her? Hug her or something? Lane's shoulders shake. Willa reaches out one very unsure hand to pat her arm, and then Lane snorts. In laughter. "What are you—" Willa says, bewildered, hand still suspended in midair.

"I just can't stop thinking about your face when you fell off the boat." Lane lifts her face; her eyes are bright. "Every time I look at you, it's just—" She makes a face, eyes wide and mouth flapping, apparently an imitation of Willa's face pre-near-death experience, then dissolves into loud laughter. "God, I'm sorry; it's not funny. You almost drowned but—" She snorts again, from holding back another bout of laughter.

Willa struggles to find an emotion to settle on and stutters through a reply. "I— Well. That's very— Maybe if you— I don't—"

"Whew." Lane leans back in her chair and wipes tears from her eyes. "God, I haven't laughed like that in *years.*"

Willa is struck, in this terrible and embarrassing moment, by how beautiful Lane is when she smiles. It's something Lane hasn't really done around Willa. It lights up her whole face, brightens her eyes and blushes her cheeks and blooms dimples at the corners of her full lips. It adds insult to injury: laughing at Willa's misfortune and looking beautiful while she does it.

"Well, it'll be a real hoot when the same thing happens during the race," Willa says, voice sharp with sarcasm and irritation. "Since I'm on my own now."

"Wait." Lane sobers quickly. "You're not seriously still doing the race after that?"

"Of course I am," Willa says, and why wouldn't she? "Just because I messed up? I mess up all the time, big deal."

Lane considers this with her eyebrows drawn flat, as if she can't wrap her head around that at all. She goes silent for a long time, then flicks her gaze away, deep in thought. Instead of chattering pointlessly, Willa drinks her lemonade and allows the quiet to settle between them. The sounds of the restaurant press around them, the happy buzz of conversation from people enjoying their meals and time together, the clink of glasses being set down, the scrape of silverware against ceramic, the whoosh of the front door being opened, and then the seashell wind chime clacking musically.

She bets Lane has never made a mistake in her life. That's probably why she doesn't date; she's holding out for just the right, perfect person. That's probably why she looks at Willa as if she's a walking disaster. Or maybe that's because Willa doesn't let anyone else see her for who she really is, and who she really is, is kind of a mess. And why would perfect Lane want to bother with her at all?

"All right, let's go out again."

Willa blinks. "What?"

Lane's eyebrows lift and fall. "On the water. I'll take you out again."

"Oh," Willa says. *On the water.* "Really?"

"I don't know, I—" Lane says, the far-off look in her eyes returning. "I really loved it, once upon a time. Sailing. And now it's—"

"Complicated," Willa fills in.

Lane's gaze refocuses, intent on Willa in a new way. "Yeah. I guess I'm not used to complicated."

"Well, maybe we're not so different then," Willa says, seizing on a way to connect with Lane and keep her around—for training purposes, of course. "Maybe you can find your love for it again through me. Teaching me, I mean."

Lane studies her for a very long moment. Willa feels pinned to her chair, unable to so much as breathe. "Maybe."

CH. *12*

WILLA'S SECOND ATTEMPT AT LEARNING to sail starts like the first; Lane picks her up in the morning, gets annoyed that Willa takes too long, and becomes uncomfortable at the sight of Bodhi shuffling around the cottage—though this time she is fully clothed. They drive in silence to Lane's parents' house again; their walk down to the boat slip is once again only punctuated by the thump of their feet landing hollowly on the dock. This time, though, the weather is sunny and cool with a breeze that hints at spring. And this time, too, Lane takes the lead, tying the sails, untying the anchoring rope, and steering the boat into the calm waters of the sound.

"You need to be aware of where the wind is coming from," Lane says, as the boat slides smoothly beneath willow branches draped into the water, light then shadow then light. "It's crucial for positioning the sails correctly and for where to sit." The sail billows to the left, while Lane sits to the right, leaning back with her strong legs pushed against the other side. The line for the mainsail is wrapped tightly around one of her hands, and the pole for the tiller is held steady in the other. "And remember that steering is opposite: Move the tiller to the left and you go right, to the right and you go left. Moving stern to port means the bow is actually starboard. Like driving a car in reverse."

"I don't drive," Willa says, petulant because she's anxious.

Lane's mouth flattens. "Never?'

In truth, her mom did teach her how to drive, in the crappy old sedan that ran on a prayer and junkyard parts. Willa shrugs. "Not recently."

Lane at the helm of the boat looks confident and relaxed, as if sailing a boat is easier for her than breathing. All Willa can think, as every muscle in her body clenches in fear of tumbling overboard, is that the race is next month and she has to cram years of sailing experience into four weeks and five days.

They pass under more low-hanging trees, coming around the northern tip of the island, and then the wide-open ocean comes into view, blue-gray and sun-speckled with short, white-peaked waves. "We're gonna tack now." Lane plants her feet more firmly on the side of the boat and leans back. "The wind is coming onto port so we're turning into it. We'll be starboard then, which means we'll need to switch sides and adjust the sails." Lane serenely watches the sky and the water, waiting for something instinctual that Willa can't understand. Then the wind catches differently in the sails, the boat arcs to the right, and Lane calls, "now," moving herself and Willa out of the way just as the boom sweeps across to the other side.

Radiant, Lane smiles up at the sun, and Willa swallows the bile climbing her throat. Sunshine engulfs them. The wind is a living thing, breathing in and out against the sails, thrumming against the lines and ropes, curling itself around Willa's body, and ruffling through her hair. Around them the ocean looks infinite and their boat so, so small.

"Are you scared?" Lane's voice is loud and carried off quickly by the wind.

"Yep," Willa says. She closes her eyes.

"Come on, it's okay," says the wind as Lane's voice. And then she's crawling over Willa's lap and perching on her other side. Her hand covers Willa's and guides it to the tiller. "Harder to screw it up once you've made it out here," Lane keeps her hand placed securely over Willa's as they steer the boat together.

"I'm sure I'll find a way," Willa replies, and Lane laughs, though it doesn't seem mean. Willa swallows down acid, takes a shaky breath, and opens her eyes. Lane isn't wrong; the waves are relatively calm, and they're heading in a straight path toward the horizon. There is so much space on the open sea that a nervous push too far just means the boat lurches and wobbles but otherwise stays upright with both occupants safely inside. There are a few other boats out: some recreational motorboats, a couple small fishing boats near shore, a commercial liner way off in the distance, but they all seem miles away.

"Let's trim the jib so we can go a bit faster." Lane reaches for line.

Willa eyes her nervously. "Do we want to go faster?"

"Well, in a race you ideally want to go fast, yes."

Lane releases Willa's hand, does something with the jib, and the boat does pick up speed. The sails pull taught and smooth with very little flapping. One of the motorboats is zipping around in wide circles ahead of them, far still, but getting closer.

"Try steering around them."

Willa shakes her head.

"Just a nudge to left."

Willa shakes her head harder. The quicker pace of the little sailboat makes the reckless, loud path of the motorboat draw nearer and nearer. Willa's hand on the tiller is sweaty, and her stomach is in turmoil.

"Willa." Lane says, her tone a warning. "Turn the boat."

"Okay." She doesn't.

The motorboat growls, zigzagging recklessly, and the little sailboat glides on, unaware of impending disaster. The sea will swallow them without a care, and Willa wants to turn, so badly, but she can't, she can't, she *can't.*

"Willa. *Turn the boat.*"

Lane's tone leaves no room for disagreement, jarring Willa out of her panic. She pushes the jib, just a little, opposite the direction she wants to go, like driving a car in reverse. The motorboat zips across their path, Willa holds her breath, and then the bow turns port, away from its chaotic path.

"Okay," Lane says, "Okay, good. That was good." Willa can hear how shaken she is despite her reassuring words.

I did it, Willa thinks, then offers the tiller back to Lane, carefully climbs over her, and leans over the side of the boat to vomit. *I really did it.*

Lane takes over fully, and with the boat in her competent hands while she patiently explains everything she does, Willa begins to relax. The ocean is gently rocking waves and smooth valleys; the sky is clear blue and endless and painted with wisps of white. A flock of cormorants circles overhead looking for fish. Willa understands in a new way why so many people spend weekends and holidays out on the water, why someone like Lane would commit so much time and energy to it, why Jenn and Robin would pack up their big city lives and sink everything into a little sailing shop on a little island off the coast of North Carolina.

"If we kept going straight, right now, what's the first land mass we'd hit?"

Lane eyes her suspiciously. "Bermuda, I guess…"

"That sounds good." Willa watches the birds circle and dive. "Just drop me there."

Lane doesn't respond; the birds fly off en masse.

How difficult would it be to change her name and start a new life in Bermuda?

"I bet everyone would be more understanding than you think," Lane says finally. "If you came clean."

Willa's experiences with human nature suggest otherwise. "I doubt it."

Lane looks at her for a long, considering moment, then back toward the horizon. "I was always good at sailing, just naturally. It came easy to me."

"Okay," Willa says, seems like a weird time to brag, but, whatever.

"I sailed because it was easy and I was good at it and it made my parents happy." Lane pauses and tugs at a rope. "So things I'm not already good at? I don't even try. Dating, for example. Starting a new career. Coaching someone."

"You were…" Willa starts, *fine*, dying on her lips. "I'm probably not easy to coach."

Lane shrugs. "The point is, you're out here doing something you aren't good at and it's something that scares you, even. So maybe you're not giving yourself enough credit."

It's not that she's afraid, though, of what people might think. "What if I lose everything?"

Lane's mouth tips into a wry grin. "You'll survive. You're young; you'll start over."

As pep talks go, it's not the most inspiring. "Right."

"You figure out who you really are," Lane says. "When you hit rock bottom."

But Willa doesn't want to hit rock bottom. She doesn't want to lose everything and she doesn't want to start over. She likes her life. Most of it. Usually. Or like, the parts that she's very carefully curated and clung to with near-desperation.

"And who are *you* really?" Willa says.

Lane looks away, eyes scanning the ocean as if she's searching for something in particular in the movement of the waves. "These days? No one."

CH. *13*

OVER THE NEXT FEW WEEKS Willa amasses an impressive collection of popular Instagram posts for her personal page and for Lane's shiny new real estate page and collects several minor sailing injuries: the bruise on her hip from slipping on the deck, then a red, angry lash across her face from a loose rope whipping out of her grip, a twisted ankle after gracelessly falling onto the dock. Her hands turn raw and cracked from pulling lines; her lips are chapped from the wind. Every muscle is tender and aching from the strain she's putting her body through. Now, whenever someone asks how her shoulder injury is holding up, the groan and wince she gives in response isn't even fake.

Willa makes slow and unsteady progress. She's still prone to panicking and making stupid mistakes, and Lane is still impatient and temperamental. And though their conversations remain stagnant, silence interspersed with orders mingled with occasional open honesty, Willa finds a new side to Lane. On the water she lets some of her walls down; that haughty lift of her chin lowers and the tense set of her shoulders and jaw eases. Everything Lane does on the water is confident and competent, and, as the weather warms, Willa gets to see more of the strong, athletic body Lane has cultivated through her years of full-time sailing. Lane on the water, helming a boat—confident, happy, strong—unsettles Willa in a way she tries to ignore.

Every time Lane snaps at her, pulling Willa's attention from a muscle pushed taut on Lane's thigh or her knotted bicep, Willa is relieved, then embarrassed.

It's annoying, Willa tells herself when her mind wanders at work or at night in bed, unable to stop thinking about something Lane said in her deep, commanding voice or the way her hair shines and billows in the breeze or the muscles in Lane's back revealed the day she wore a tank top, and how Willa nearly capsized the boat that day.

When Willa can raise the sails and launch from a dock on her own, they switch to the marina adjacent to the store and to the boat Willa borrowed from Mr. Kelley. When she manages that without any catastrophic incidents, Lane nods and says, "Well, safe to say you won't kill yourself immediately." After that, Lane doesn't call again. Willa is desperate to stop thinking about her.

*   *   *

THE FIRST BONFIRE OF THE year is at Hunter's place, on the section of private beach near the condo Hunter's parents bought for her. Willa and Bodhi don their best flip-flops and walk up to the beachfront neighborhood of shingle-sided duplexes laced with white-washed balconies and rooftop decks.

"It's not like I expected us to be best friends," Willa says as they follow smoke and thumping music past the grassy dunes. "But sometimes she's nice and sometimes she's not, and I think I just can't figure her out. It's driving me crazy and—"

"Hey," Hunter says as she jogs up. She hands Bodhi a beer and walks with them to the fire, where a dozen or so people are sitting on blankets or standing around talking. "Who are you talking about?"

"This chick Wills is into," Bodhi says, casually sipping foam from the lid of her beer can.

"What. I am *not*."

"Ooh," Hunter interjects, before Willa can craft a better rebuttal. "Who is it?" She looks around, as if it's one of the people they hang out with.

"Some older lady," Bodhi says. "She's hot though."

Willa rolls her eyes and retrieves a drink from the blue cooler parked up the beach near a wooden stairwell, since Hunter only hand-delivers drinks to Bodhi. And anyway, first of all, Lane is only fourteen years older than her, hardly some old lady. Second of all, she isn't hot. Not regular hot. Like, annoying hot. *If* Willa thought about her that way, which she *doesn't*. Except for her muscles, and her lips, and her long neck, and her eyes. But only, like, *objectively*. Third, Willa is definitely not at all obsessed with her. That's why, when Lane comes striding purposefully down the wooden stairs as if Willa conjured her up out her own swirling, frustrated thoughts, Willa is utterly dumbfounded.

"Lane?"

Lane pauses at the bottom step, head cocked. She spots Willa, looks her up and down, and says, in a bored voice, "Ah. Of course you're here."

Of course *she* is. This is her sort-of friend's party. "Why are *you* here?" Someone like Lane surely isn't here for a what they loosely call a party but is really just an excuse to get drunk and smoke weed on the beach before hooking up with the people they usually hook up with or to gossip about the people who are getting drunk, smoking weed, and hooking up with each other.

"I'm here to get the music turned down. It's deafening."

Willa is relieved and mortified in equal measure. "It's not that loud," she says, trying to head Lane off at the pass before she stomps off to lecture someone.

"It is that loud. I have to work in the morning." She steps onto the beach and around Willa. "*Some of us* have jobs."

Sometimes it feels as if they'll never move past that day when Willa first ran into Lane, and that first social-media-obsessed, beach-bum-slacker impression Willa made on her.

"I have a job," Willa points out, scrambling to follow. "You've seen me at my job." Lane crosses her arms and takes a few more steps. "Wait. You live over here?" She been at this beach and at Hunter's house hundreds of times. Has she seen Lane before? Willa is sure she'd remember her.

"Yes." Lane's chin lifts higher. "Though I'm typically sleeping at this hour like most sane people."

Willa ignores the slight. "Well, these parties happen like all the time. Honestly, they're pretty chill." After hesitating for a moment, knowing that she won't, Willa adds, "Why don't you hang out for a little?"

Lane gives a sharp laugh. "Yeah, right—"

"Wills, how long does it take to get a damn beer." Bodhi stumbles up though the sand. She lost her shirt sometime in the last few minutes, and is dressed in only shorts and a bikini top even though it's chilly still, particularly near the water. She throws her arms around Willa and kisses her cheek with a loud *mwah*! Tipsy Party Bodhi is extremely affectionate. She seems to realize that Lane is standing there but doesn't seem to notice her crossed arms and tensely set shoulders. "Oh, dude, hey! We were just talking about you. Crazy."

In the dark, Lane's face is inscrutable. "Were you?" she says, in an equally unreadable tone. Bodhi, for whatever reason, probably her cavalier attitude toward clothing and working and relationships and… everything, seems to make Lane uncomfortable. She stopped getting out of the car when picking Willa up for sailing lessons.

"Just sailing stuff. In general, you know." Willa can feel the confused look Bodhi gives her. "Anyway, Bo can you turn the music down? Lane has to work in the morning."

Bodhi raises her beer bottle in salute and trots off to find the source of the music. Willa turns to apologize for the interruption when the bonfire flares with the sudden burst and crackle of a new log thrown on the flames, and Lane's face is illuminated in the orange glow. She watches Lane watch Bodhi, who is laughing and saying something with one arm stretched up and behind her head, and Willa realizes that *uncomfortable* isn't quite what Lane is feeling for Bodhi after all. The fire down the beach pops and flares, and irrational, surprising jealousy burns in Willa's chest. *Why Bodhi*, she thinks as Lane walks away, though she knows the answer. Why does Bodhi coast by, handed everything, wanted by everyone, while Willa has to fight and fumble and fail, over and over. Why doesn't Lane like her? Why doesn't Lane look at *her* like that? Because Lane is into Bodhi, and Willa wants it to be her.

Oh, crap, she is into Lane.

CH. *14*

"What? Do I look weird or something?"

It's the third time Bodhi has caught her staring this afternoon. *If only,* Willa thinks. "No, sorry. I'm just distracted today." Willa straightens a display of sunscreen and tries to stop her mind from slipping to thoughts of Lane—and Lane and Bodhi—again.

"I bet you're itching to get back out on the water," Robin says, peering over the top of her glasses and tapping her inventory sheet. "In fact, maybe you should take some time off, Willa."

"Oh, yes." Jenn comes behind Willa at the register and squeezes her shoulders affectionately. "You should be training as much as possible! We want you to win this thing, for all of us!" Jenn shoos Willa away from the register and tells her to take all the time she needs, as Bodhi mutters, "Jeez, no pressure, Ma."

But it's not as if Willa doesn't already know she's carrying the weight of an island's worth of expectations. Thanks to Lane's sailing lessons, she isn't totally hopeless but she has yet to venture out on her own and hasn't managed a successful supervised run where she handles everything herself.

As she has several times since her last lesson with Lane, Willa slinks off to the marina and sits in her borrowed boat, still anchored to the dock. Mr. Kelley, busy as always running the marina by himself, leaves her to it, never watching her or commenting on the fact that she's very unlikely to win a boat race while anchored to the dock. She curls up on the bow with her legs tucked against her chest and her arms wrapped around her knees. It's warm during the daylight hours now. It has been for a while. The race is imminent, and Willa's doom is impending.

When she was a kid, Willa told her classmates that her dad was in the military, a high-ranking officer in a highly top-secret mission. "We never know where he is," Willa would say. "Sometimes we don't hear from him for months." And those things were true, though not because he was serving the country. She wonders now, watching the sun-drenched water lap up the sides of her boat, if she'd just been honest in the first place, about everything, how much that would have changed things. She's had to keep up the ruses for years, remembering the lies she'd told and keeping her fake stories straight. Her senior year of high school she told people her parents had split, recently, and that's why her mom was remarrying and her dad wouldn't be at graduation. She's tired. She doesn't want to lie to the people who care about her. She wishes she was a different person. If she'd just been honest from the start, that it was just her and her mom and it always had been, it could have been over and done with, and she could have just been herself all along. And maybe someone could like her, the real her.

But it's too late for that.

Willa takes a photo, tilting the camera and leaning close so the ocean stretches out, infinite and incomprehensible. She puts a dark filter over it and captions, *"What would an ocean be without a monster lurking in the dark? It would be like sleep without dreams."*

Lane and Bodhi make sense. They have a lot in common, and Bodhi is laid back where Lane is high-strung, and they'd probably bring out the best in each other. The wind stirs Willa's hair; the boat sways from side to side. Bodhi is her best friend, more her sister than the little girl her mom had with a man Willa barely knows. She can be jealous of everything Bodhi has, and is, while still wanting the best for her. Willa stares at the blue sky, more endless even than the sea, and allows herself to feel small and insignificant and sad for a moment, before climbing out of the boat and getting on with it.

The same exuberant receptionist greets Willa at the real estate office, but this time Lane is there and calls her in right away.

"I just saw your Instagram post. Have you been going out and practicing a lot? How's it going?" Lane is so uncharacteristically excited that Willa very nearly lies and tells her that it's been going great and she's been out all the time.

"It's not."

Lane's face falls, then pulls into its more usual tight lines. "Why not?"

"Well," Willa sits in a soft, armless chair. "If I drown, no one will be there to pull me out."

"You're aren't going to drown," Lane says, and Willa hopes it's the beginning of a very encouraging pep talk. "That's what a life jacket is for."

Willa frowns and looks down at her lap. There is no life jacket buoyant enough to save her now. She's always been honest with Lane, the most herself anyone has seen, and Lane doesn't like her. That's proof enough for Willa that she has to carry on with the competition no matter how afraid or unprepared she is. "Wait, you follow my Instagram?"

"Yeah, you agreed to promote me remember?" Lane says before Willa can get her hopes up that it means something.

"Right."

"I got some new clients from that, by the way. Haven't sold anything. But still."

Lane has saved her ass twice now, literally and figuratively, and despite her gruff demeanor has been for there for Willa and helped her despite very little personal gain. She owes Lane this, more than promo for a job Lane doesn't even seem to like. More than that, though, she likes Lane and wants her to be happy, even if that comes at the cost of Willa's happiness. She can give her this.

Willa sighs and says what she came there to say. "Well, I wanted to thank you for your help and take you out and buy you a drink."

Lane leans away. "Oh, I don't think— That— That's not necessary." Her cheeks darken.

It's exactly what Willa thought she would say. "It's nothing big. Just some of us stopping by The Oyster Bar tonight around eight, and if you wanted to come by for a bit…" Lane starts to shake her head again. "Bodhi will be there," Willa adds. Her insides twist, and jealousy thrums against her chest like a heartbeat, but still she smiles. "Come on, just one drink. Please?"

Lane pretends that all of this is of no interest to her; she shuffles through some papers on her desk, reads over one with her mouth set firm. But Willa can see the deep pink on her cheeks and the way her eyes dart around, landing on nothing.

"Um. Well that's—" Lane scowls, seemingly to get ahold of herself. "I'll see if I have a few minutes to drop by."

Her plan is to convince Bodhi to go out for drinks, hang out until Lane arrives, and then make some excuse to leave early. With her extra time off, Willa goes home to crawl into bed with her laptop and whatever junk food they have at the cottage, binge watch terrible reality TV shows full of terrible people, and drown in self-pity. Her phone rings before she even makes it inside. It's her grandparents— which one she never knows, as they only have a landline. Willa answers while unlocking the door, juggling her keys and phone and skateboard.

"Yeah?" She drops her skateboard and curses. Whichever grandparent is on the other line tsks. "Sorry. Hello?"

"Willa. It's your grandmother." Her grandparents are not without kindness and in fact have been very generous to her over the years. After all, they could have kicked her out long ago or raised her rent to what it should be, which is well out of Willa's budget. But they have never quite let go of the notion that it was Willa who got her mom's life so far off track so young, forcing them to come to the rescue twenty-two years ago.

"Hi, Grandma," Willa says, fake-chirpy, pacing the living room. "How are you?"

"I'm fine; I'm fine," her grandmother says, brusque at first, then remembers her manners. "How are you, Willa?"

"I'm well." She walks and turns, walks and turns. Her grandparents do not call to chat. "So, what's going on? Everything okay?"

*   *   *

WILLA BREAKS THE NEWS TO Bodhi over drinks. The Oyster Bar is quiet tonight, just a handful of regulars. Soon enough it will be packed with tourists, and by then, Willa doesn't know where she'll be or *how* she'll be, post-race.

"Three weeks isn't terrible," Bodhi says, after Willa explains that her grandparents want to rent out the cottage for spring break this year. Her grandfather has been dealing with some health problems, and her grandparents need the extra money. Guilt and frustration war inside Willa; she wants her grandfather to be okay, of course, but she doesn't want to scramble to find somewhere to stay. Not right now.

"Just wish it wasn't the three weeks right before the race. Like, I'd go visit my mom, but…" She wouldn't anyway, actually, but now she can't even if she did want to.

"Yeah." Bodhi spins on her chair and looks around. "Didn't you say a bunch of people were coming?" Willa shrugs. She did say that. "Anyway, I'll probably just stay with Hunter. You could too."

Willa makes a face. First, she knows without confirming it that Bodhi and Hunter are still sleeping together and two, Willa finds Hunter irritating after about three minutes. Three weeks would be— "Nah. I'll figure something out."

They order a second drink and talk about a friend who got a job offer in Raleigh and is leaving the island. Then Bodhi starts to get restless, and Willa is sure that Lane isn't going to stop by at all. She's relieved, then guilty about being relieved, then mad all over again that it's Bodhi who caught Lane's eye and not her, that Bodhi already has so many people to choose from and the *one time* that Willa likes someone—

"Hey, it's your sailing coach again. Man, she's everywhere lately."

Willa looks up, and her heart stutters. She makes an excuse to leave and somehow manages to walk home and not right into the ocean.

CH. *15*

As the days get warmer, the sail shop gets busier. Willa pulls as many shifts as possible, despite Robin and Jenn's insistence that she can take as much time as she needs to practice. But Bodhi is out somewhere more often than not these days, and someone needs to be at the shop. She'd also rather not think about what Bodhi and Lane might be up to. On the night that Willa left Lane and Bodhi at the Oyster Bar, Bodhi didn't come home until two a.m., disheveled and flushed, and Willa slammed her bedroom door closed harder than she'd meant to. They haven't spoken at all since then. And anyway, working a lot also means she doesn't have to worry about the race or finding a place to stay during spring break. It's easier to tell herself that things will be fine if she barely has time to think about it all.

One week before she has to be out of the cottage, Willa passes long lines of cars and mostly full hotel parking lots on her way into work. The pavement is hot beneath the soles of her Vans. Soon the island will be packed to the brim with tourists, and by then Willa will have either completed the race successfully or ruined her life completely. At least the whole thing will be over, one way or another.

The customers come nearly non-stop, not a long line of them, but there's not a moment all day when she or Robin or Jenn aren't busy helping one person with customers milling around in the store or impatiently waiting their turn to be helped. Willa is helping someone decide on a rash guard that blocks UV rays, while Robin searches the store for an item she can't seem to find.

"I'm not sure…" Robin says, brows furrowed as she flips through one rack, then another. "Spinlock, you said?" The customer nods, and Robin's brows pinch tighter.

Willa apologizes to the customer she's helping, saying that she'll be right back, and pops over to take a guess. "The Rig-Sense?" It's a product she was sent recently to promote on her Instagram, a new type of rig tension device used to measure the line tension on small boats. "It's right over here," she says, leading the customer to where the devices are hung on a hook. She directs the customer buying a rash guard to the register and on the way, pulls down a Rig-Sense. "Do you already have the app? It's such a great way to log your rig settings…"

The days are getting longer now; the island is flush with daylight. By the time the store closes and Willa cashes out the register, the sun is just starting to set, dancing pink and orange across the ocean waves. She doesn't really want to go home. Though she doubts Bodhi will be there, she isn't in the mood to take that chance. Avoiding Lane has been easier, though Willa both dreads and hopes they'll eventually run into each other. She hesitates outside the store long enough that Robin and Jenn catch up to her after locking up.

"What a day!" Robin says, making a *whew* gesture across her forehead.

"And what would we have done without you, hmm?" Jenn smiles and smooths Willa's hair in a motherly gesture that makes affection blossom in Willa's chest.

"Ah, well." She ducks her head blushing. "You have Bodhi."

"Yes." Robin and Jenn exchange a glance. "We do have Bodhi. Who we love! Very much. But who is…"

"Bodhi," Robin fills in.

It makes Willa chuckle, the exasperated affection. She knows it well. In fact, she should probably get home and try to catch Bodhi between her hookups and kayaking trips and hiking excursions and wake boarding and partying to make up with her. Willa has no claim on Lane and therefore no right to be jealous. It's not Bodhi's fault that she's, well, Bodhi.

"I should prob—" Willa starts, speaking at the same time as Robin.

"Sorry. I was just saying, we haven't had a chance to see you in action."

"Action?" Willa squints; the sun has dipped low enough to be right at sight line, blinding her as she looks at the women.

"Yes, since you've been sailing again, training for the race. We're just so excited!" Jenn clasps her hands in front of her and leans over, as if she's sharing a secret. "Could we get a little preview?"

For a flash, Willa wants to blurt out the truth. Robin and Jenn's unwarranted belief in her seizes Willa's lungs, squeezing at her heart. How could she lie to them, these two people who have been nothing but kind and supportive, who treat her no differently than their own daughter? Who have faith in her, a person who is not at all who she claims to be, when they really shouldn't. But would they understand that Willa didn't lie because she wanted to trick them, but because she so badly wants to be that person whom they see?

"Sure," Willa hears herself saying, with a fake confidence she's gotten much too good at. "I'd love to show you."

Somehow, with Jenn and Robin's eager eyes watching, Willa is able to do what she hasn't been able to do in weeks. She climbs aboard her little borrowed boat, pulls lines and tightens rigs and raises the mainsail without incident. She's slow and little awkward, but she manages just fine. Willa checks the rudder, finds the wind direction, adjusts the tension in the sails, loops the anchor from the dock. Somehow, it's as if Lane is with her, guiding her hand as she steers carefully out of the marina. It's Lane's steady, no-nonsense voice that keeps her from clipping another boat that's moored at the end of the dock, Lane's imagined solid presence that steadies Willa's grip on the lines as she steers out into the open waters.

Jenn and Robin whoop and cheer from the dock. It would almost be enough, their joy, this genuine moment, even if Willa doesn't win the race. Almost. She sails far enough away that Robin and Jenn become dark silhouettes on the dock, then makes a wobbly turn and heads back.

Bodhi isn't at the cottage when Willa makes it home after dark; no bike is parked in her spot and no lights are on. But an impeccably detailed white SUV is parked on the curb.

"Hey."

"Hey." Lane makes her way down the packed-sand driveway and up the stairs until she's tucked under the porch light next to Willa. "I guess you didn't get my text?"

Willa put her phone in her backpack before her little sailing demonstration and forgot to check it after. She pulls it out to find a text from Lane that simply reads "coming by" so she isn't sure what difference it would have made, really.

"Come on in." Willa unlocks the door and steps inside, flipping on the bright light in the foyer, but Lane doesn't follow.

"Actually..." She slips a bag off her shoulder and holds it out. "I just wanted to drop this off." When Willa takes it in confusion, she adds, "It's just some of my old sailing gear. Since you don't have any of your own I thought— I mean Bodhi probably has some stuff you could borrow, but—" Bodhi's name on Lane's lips makes something sour curdle in Willa's stomach.

"Thanks. I'll get it back to you when the race is done."

Willa doesn't manage to keep the sourness from her voice, and it seems to bring Lane up short. Her eyes scan Willa's face, then settle at her own feet. "No. Keep it. Um."

Willa is confounded. The gesture is kind and generous, but Lane seems almost chagrined, as if the gear was merely a segue into something else.

And then, of course, it dawns on Willa. "Bodhi's not here. But I can track her down."

She figured that Lane and Bodhi would have exchanged numbers at least, though it wouldn't be the first time Bodhi has slept with someone and soon thereafter became a ghost. She may be jealous and bitter, but Bodhi is still her best friend and she still cares about Lane. "The thing is, Bo is like the ocean." Lane gives her a puzzled look. "Beautiful and free and impossible to contain."

Lane's eyes narrow. "Okay…"

"Okay, well. Thanks for the gear. Goodnight." She starts to close the door, making a mental note to tell Bodhi that she needs to take Lane out on a proper date. Someone like Lane isn't going to be okay with catching Bodhi's attention whenever the wind blows or when Bodhi doesn't have something more interesting going on. She's not Hunter.

"Wait, Willa."

Willa pauses with the door half-shut, and Lane opens her mouth to stay something, but doesn't. She just blinks again and shakes her head and says, "Nothing. Never mind. If I don't see you before, then…" That look again, something in Lane's eyes, something more, that Willa can't sort out. "Um. Good luck at the race."

CH. *16*

"Hey, it's Willa. Again. Still wondering if I could crash with you for a bit? Call me if you get this soon."

Willa packs her backpack, rolls her pillow into her sleeping bag, and makes a few more desperate phone calls. As Porter Island prepares for an onslaught of tourists, everyone she knows has disappeared. She shouldn't be surprised, as a lot of the locals tend to go elsewhere for spring break—why stick around and deal with the traffic and packed beaches and long waits at every restaurant and bar and gas station when they don't have to—yet for some reason she assumed *someone* would be here. She tries Bodhi again, desperate enough to take her up on the offer to stay at Hunter's, but the two of them left to sail up the chain of Outer Banks islands yesterday and are camping on one of the undeveloped islands where there is no cell reception or Internet access.

"Crap." Willa stuffs some protein bars into the front pocket of her backpack just as the front door clicks and jiggles; someone is turning a key in the deadbolt. "Crap, crap."

Willa grabs a phone charger and some cash, double checks that the trunk holding all of her worldly possessions is locked and tucked away under the bed, then dashes out the sliding glass back door just as a family with Midwestern accents and way too much oversized luggage bangs their way inside. She throws her bag over the deck railing, then her sleeping bag, and then jumps over herself, landing in the soft sand not quite delicately. She was supposed to be out of the cottage last night and she knows this family will tour the place inside and out, oohing over what they like and making note for their future complaints about anything they don't. She has just enough time to take a #morningview picture beneath her favorite loblolly tree before she hears the sliding door scrape open. She's three doors down before she realizes she forgot to grab her skateboard from the carport.

At some point, Willa hopes, she will learn to plan ahead, be practical, perhaps even take care of something important before her back is against the wall and she is out of options, but for now she just has a series of *if onlys* to work with.

If only she had asked to stay at a friend's place sooner. If only she hadn't already told Robin and Jenn she was set and didn't need to stay with them. If only she had found a second job when the sail shop was slow and saved some money for a hotel. If only she had booked a cheap room way back when there were rooms available. If only her boat had a cabin. If only she'd asked Bodhi if she could use her boat, which does have a cabin. If only she'd never signed up for this stupid race in the first place and could have left the island instead of staying on and pretending to train for the race. If only she wasn't the human embodiment of accidentally making a toilet overflow at someone else's house with no idea of how to stop the disaster, what to do about it, or how to tell anyone what happened.

"Hey, it's Willa. Again…"

Backpack slung over one arm, sleeping bag gripped in the other, Willa heads toward the sail shop. Without her skateboard, the few miles there seem unending. The pavement is hot, and the air is thick and sticky. Jenn and Robin are both working today; they usually do on Sundays when the store is open shorter hours, so Willa plans to swallow her pride and tell them that she does need a place to stay then stash her stuff at the store and sit on her boat for a while. When she finally makes it to the main road near the row of busy restaurants, however, the sky has filled with heavy gray clouds. Near the upscale hotels, the wind pushes against her, and she picks up her pace. By the time she makes it to the section of condominiums near Hunter's place, it's raining. In her last dash to Hunter's porch, she gets soaked. And though she knows Bodhi and Hunter aren't there, Willa pounds on the door.

Crap.

She probably should have checked the weather forecast, though that would involve having foresight and not being an idiot, so of course she wasn't prepared for rain. With no choice but to wait it out on the porch, Willa sinks to the ground, huddled in a dirty corner with her damp backpack and sleeping bag clutched to her chest. Her phone is mercifully dry, but no one has called or messaged back. *When was the last time Hunter swept her porch,* Willa wonders, kicking at a cobweb filled with dead leaves and deader bugs. She has to keep the cottage clean or her grandparents will never let her hear the end of it. That's the difference, she supposes, between being allowed to borrow something instead of having it handed to her on a silver platter. *What does Bodhi see in Hunter,* Willa thinks, flicking away an old cigarette butt. What does Bodhi see in anyone? Lane, for instance.

Someone in a hooded black coat and waterproof boots passes on the sidewalk. Willa tracks their journey to the kiosk that houses dozens of little metal mailboxes. They collect their mail and head back, head down. Willa's sure the sail shop sells that brand of coat, the boots too. It's not just rain gear but foul weather gear for sailing. "Do you sail?" She wants to yell through the clatter of heavy rain. "Want to take my place in a very prestigious race? Want to take my name, assume my identity, and take over my crappy life while you're at it?" But she says nothing.

"What are you doing here?" The person in the coat stops, staring at her. Lane's face peers out from beneath the hood.

Willa expected Lane's home to have a vibe similar to her parents' mausoleum-esque house, only smaller. But as Lane ushers her in and goes off in search of a towel, she discovers that Lane's place is cozy and warm and modern, thoughtfully put together the way Willa imagines she would do in her own home. The condo layout is just like Hunter's with a large living area, a small kitchen leading to a small deck, and a bedroom and bathroom down a short hallway. The furniture looks new: a squashy brown leather couch, a round table by a large window, a big shelf on one wall that's painted white, and another matching shelf that holds a TV and a record player. The walls are painted in various off-white hues: almost-beige in the living room, just a hint of green tint in the kitchen, eggshell in the hallway, pale gray in the bathroom, and, in what little Willa can see of the one bedroom, the faintest hint of light, light blue. Instead of the cold, untouched feel of the Cordova's huge house, it has the vibe of someone who has had years to cultivate their taste, to select just the right decor pieces and furniture, the feel of someone who has, over time, gathered enough accouterments and knickknacks to fill shelves and drawers and collect on tabletops, unlike Willa, whose personal items more or less fit in the damp bag at her feet, who has to be ready to pack her all of her things and disappear for weeks or months.

"Here." Lane frowns as she hands Willa a towel.

"Oh, I'm allowed to use the white towels here?" Willa says, pressing it to her cheek.

Lane's mouth twitches. "Yeah. It's fine. So. What were you doing out there?"

The answer to that is complicated and doesn't paint Willa in the best light, so Willa gives the easy answer, "I was walking and got caught in the rain."

Lane's eyebrows raise. "Walking... with a sleeping bag?"

Willa glances at her sleeping bag. It's splotched with wet spots and unfurled in a heap on the floor. "Well, I—" *Was off to a slumber party,* her brain supplies, but she isn't ten so that's probably not going to work. *Was going to meet Bodhi; we're camping. Love that great outdoors!* But she doesn't love the great outdoors and she doesn't really want to talk about Bodhi with Lane anymore or ever again. So she's left with nothing but the truth. "My grandparents own the beach cottage I live in. They rent it out in the summer and this year they decided to rent

73

it out for spring break too." Willa loops the towel over her head like a headscarf. "And I sort of have nowhere to stay at the moment."

"Hmm." Lane sets her hands on her hips, scans Willa's face, then unzips her coat and pulls off her boots. "You can stay here, if you want."

"I—" The towel slips off Willa's head and onto the floor. "Really?"

"Sure. Unless you'd rather sleep out on the porch?"

"Not really, no."

Lane nods, as though that's that. No big deal. Willa can just… sleep in her home. See Lane's bed and shower and what she looks like first thing in the morning, soft and rumpled with sleep and— "The couch pulls out. Bathroom's down there." Lane pads over to the kitchen. "And pick up that towel, please. Are you hungry?"

Willa can only blink in surprise and nod her head.

"Great, I was just about to make pancakes." Lane smiles, throwing Willa off even more. *How is this happening? And why is she letting it? Is this a dream? Hasn't she had this dream? Wasn't Lane wearing—* "Willa?"

"Yes?" It comes out as a croak, breathy and strained.

"The towel."

CH. *17*

LANE PUTTERS AROUND THE SMALL, though well-equipped, kitchen, and Willa sits at the little round table. Rain thrashes against the glass door and down past the dunes, where frothy waves hurl themselves against the dark sand. Willa hunches in on herself, damp still from getting caught in the sudden downpour and cold from a draft coming through a nearby vent.

"Here you go." Lane sets down a plate of steaming pancakes with a pat of butter beginning to ooze on top, a bottle of real maple syrup, and silverware dropped in a pile as she retrieves her own plate.

"Why?" Willa says, because she's cold and confused and not entirely sure how she ended up here, in Lane's house, eating pancakes with real maple syrup and a pat of melting butter.

Lane glances at her quizzically and sits in the chair across the table. "Why pancakes? Is that a philosophical question or?

"No, not—" Willa pulls a fork from the pile of silverware and stabs the air with it. "Not the pancakes. Why are you being so nice to me? Why let me stay here? I didn't think you even liked me." She twirls the fork around nothing, not sure why she can't just accept Lane's kindness at face value, except for the fact that is feels an awful lot like charity, as though Willa is some street urchin that Lane rescued, which she isn't, even though she sort of was— "I don't need your pity. I can find somewhere to stay."

Instead of the argument Willa braces for, Lane shrugs and says, "Okay."

Lane sets three pancakes in a circle around her plate, smooths the butter across each, and then cuts one pancake into neat, evenly divided triangles. She spears one triangle onto her fork and then squeezes one drop of syrup onto it. *Who eats pancakes like that,* Willa wonders, *and why is it kind of cute?* Willa flops out her own pancakes carelessly, pours syrup in an oozing puddle, and leaves the butter to curl and mingle with the syrup in whatever haphazard way it chooses. It feels like spite, the messiness of it in the face of Lane's orderliness, and maybe it is.

"I didn't," Lane says, after a stretch of silence.

"Didn't what?"

A triangle of pancake, a dollop of syrup. "Like you. At first." She chews and considers this with a tilt of her head. "I thought you were annoying and lazy and irresponsible and just messing with me for fun."

"Ah," Willa says, because what else can she say to that?

Lane continues her methodical pancake eating. "Even up until we got on the boat that first time, I thought you were just screwing with me. And I'd wind up on your YouTube pranking channel—"

"I'm not *twelve*," Willa interrupts. *A YouTube pranking channel, come on.*

Lane waves her fork in Willa's direction. "Right, so, it wasn't until you fell in and almost drowned that I realized you were serious. That you'd really gotten yourself into this situation with the race. And that you really, really didn't know what you were doing."

"And you thought it was hilarious," Willa points out.

"No— Well, yeah a little. But then I thought—" She chews slowly, as if working up to something. "I get it, you know? Feeling like you have something to prove. Like if you can achieve this one thing, everyone will give you the respect and love you deserve. They won't, for the record. But I get it."

"Oh," Willa says.

They finish eating, and Lane clears the table, insisting on washing the dishes while Willa finds a place to stash away her backpack and sleeping bag. The rainstorm moves out nearly as suddenly as it came in, and sunlight soon crowds into the small space of Lane's condo.

Lane comes out of the kitchen drying her hands on a dish towel; her silhouette is set aglow by the streaming sunlight. "Hey, can I take you somewhere?"

*   *   *

"SOMEWHERE" TURNS OUT TO BE a mystery journey by boat, and, instead of taking her, Lane instructs Willa where and how to sail them there, wherever *there* is, launching again from the dock behind Lane's parents' massive, empty home. They travel up the sound through the peaceful, shallow waters. It's windy enough that they don't need to raise the mainsail, and navigating through the low-lying salt marshes seems less intimidating to Willa than the open water. She knows the landscape of these islands placed in a chain like the extended string of an archer's bow. She knows the swish of the long grasses and the odd grace of long-legged blue herons and the taste of the sea and the wild green brush that passes by. It's home. And sailing it, confidently, competently, with Lane placidly staring out at the sun-speckled water, is like a missing puzzle piece finally finding its place in Willa's life.

They head north and northeast and due north. They don't speak save for Lane's instructions and tips and warnings, and once she tells Willa that any boat with more than a six-foot draft couldn't make it through the sound, and, depending on the tide, sometimes even small boats find themselves stuck. Much later, after they've passed Kitty Hawk, Willa breaks the serenity to tell Lane that she's never been this far north, only coming up to Kill Devil Hills once on a school field trip in fifth grade to see the Wright Brothers memorial.

Lane makes a noise in response that sounds like disappointment but says, "Well, it's pretty far."

When they finally pull ashore and dock, Willa is stiff and sore and badly in need of a bathroom. They've stopped at one of the barely developed islands, reachable only by boat and only navigable by four-wheel-drive off-road vehicles. The beach is wild and almost unchanged from the way it would have looked to the sailors who came ashore centuries ago. Willa is lucky to find a ranger station with a bathroom, and even then it's an outbuilding without running water. She's careful not to touch anything.

Lane waits nearby, turned away with her hands at her side and face tilted toward the sun. She's at ease out here, Willa can see, free out in the coastal wilderness just as Bodhi is. Willa pushes back at the twinge of jealousy that rises, small and ugly, at yet another thing Bodhi and Lane share.

"We can't get too close," Lane explains, though not too close to *what*. "If we carefully go up the dunes, that's probably best."

Willa's shoes fill with sand as they climb the dunes. Lane scans the beach, and they wait and wait and wait. Willa uses both hands to push her hair out her face and says, "What—" Lane lifts a hand to silence her. And they wait.

"There." Lane points. Willa squints to see blobs of something moving along the shore, just shadows hidden by more shadowing beneath the dunes. And then they come closer.

She's heard of them of course, the wild horses on this island that are believed to have originally been brought on exploring ships that likely wrecked in the shallow sandbar-prone waters in the 1500s. Somehow, the horses made it to shore and then made themselves at home. The herd meandering up the beach toward them are direct descendants of those horses: stocky and rust-colored with scattered patches of white, who have been left alone to live as free as they wish, never ridden, never tamed, never used by people for their own purposes, never forced to be something they aren't or don't want to be.

"Wow," Willa says under her breath. She lets her hair go to fly loose in the wind. "Wow."

CH. *18*

"How close can I get without scaring them?" Willa is already slide-running down the soft dune, phone out and camera ready.

"Legally, you can't go closer than fifty feet." Lane trails after, cautiously picking her way down to the beach. The horses, still a ways down, don't seem to notice their approach. There are ten of them, Willa thinks, but as they're clustered in a wandering clump and partly hidden by dunes, it's hard to say exactly how many horses are in the herd. There are two smaller ones—foals, she can tell as she gets closer—both with sandy blond manes and swishing blond tails and little white diamonds stamped on their foreheads. Willa sets her sights on them.

"Fifty feet," Lane says again, a warning. But who is really out here measuring that carefully? Who is out here to even notice— "Willa, the ranger station."

Willa skids to a stop in the sand. Right. Well, with the right angle and zoom… "I can make it look like I got closer, no problem." She takes dozens of pictures, rapid-fire, until she finally gets it just right, a close-in shot of the two foals, one with its head lifted and seeming to look right at the camera with something knowing and wise in its eyes. The horse was actually looking at two seagulls who had started squawking and carrying on nearby, but no one needs to know that. Willa selects a subtle filter to make the blue sky look bluer, the sea grass greener, the copper color of the foal's coat shinier—just a little. She captions it: *What an incredible moment with these beautiful wild horses! Never know what a sailing adventure will bring!*

Lane glances over Willa's shoulder as she's hashtagging. "Why do you do that?"

"Oh," Willa says, distracted. "It helps people find your posts. Some people follow certain hashtags or search for them." She should really give Lane an Instagram tutorial if she doesn't even know what hashtags are.

"No, I mean. Why do you make things seem like something else? Why embellish?"

Willa rolls her eyes and hits *post*. "Everyone embellishes." Lane's eyebrows furrow, and she frowns, seemingly unsatisfied with that answer. Willa sighs, petulant even to her own ears as she says, "Are you gonna give me a speech about the evils of social media and how it's turning kids these days into vain, vapid, digital zombies? Cuz I've heard it before."

"No..." Lane says, weakly. "I just—" She turns to look back at the herd, which is wandering farther away now, meandering toward the water way down the beach. "I just think that if you were honest—if you were yourself—that people would like you just as much."

"You're wrong," Willa says. "They wouldn't." Willa strides back to the dunes, intending to stomp away decisively, but the rolling hills of shifting soft sand are nearly impossible to climb, so instead she stumbles and curses and loses her footing.

"You haven't even tried."

"I don't need to."

"But how can you know—"

"I just do!" Willa loses her balance completely. She slides down and falls backward, only able to stop by dropping down and sprawling out in the sand. "I just do," she repeats, holding on to fistfuls of shifting sand. Lane sits next to her. *Why does she even care?* Lane certainly didn't like her, not until she nearly drowned *and* made her feel bad *and* after she set her up with Bodhi. She doesn't like her at all in the way Willa wants her to. Willa glances at the dune that looms impassable above her. What was the point of this trip anyway? Some avant-garde training technique meant to teach her patience and how being her true self is the real accomplishment or something cheesy like that?

They sit together in irritated silence; the horses have long since disappeared and just a gang of noisy seagulls strut in and out of the tide to keep them company.

"We should probably get ba—" Willa starts, as Lane interrupts, "It was my first—first date in..." She pushes her hair out her face and lets the sentence hang unfinished. "I haven't..."

"Haven't... What?" Willa looks over, but Lane is staring at the ocean. Willa is just about to give up on her and again suggest they leave; she's sure that Lane will pretend she said nothing, when Lane takes a deep breath.

"The date you followed me to."

"I didn't—" Willa starts, but Lane lifts an eyebrow, and she snaps her mouth shut.

"That was..." Lane full lips quirk for a just a second, then flatten. "I told myself it was because I was busy being a world champion and all, but the truth is, I was afraid. Afraid of who I was and what I wanted, so I didn't date. Not that I haven't *been* with anyone... Just not who I..." She doesn't look at Willa to gauge her reaction, to see if she's understating what Lane is trying to say, she just stares ahead. "I spent my whole life convinced that I was happy to be this illusion of a person. My identity was so tied up in what other people expected of me and by the time I realized that I had no idea what I wanted or who I really was it felt like it was too late to even try. Trust me, you're much better off just being honest. Because now it's like, have I ever been happy? Do I even know what that feels like? Did I love sailing because I like it, or was I just always expected to like it so I forced it? How can I tell?"

Willa scoops up handfuls of sand and creates a little soft pile between her sneakers. "I think you just know," she finally says, sure that being "into sailing" is code for something else. "Haven't you tried doing, like, other types of— *boating*? By now?" Meaning Bodhi. Meaning sleeping with Bodhi. Surely that would have clarified some things for her.

Lane shakes her head. "Not yet, no."

"Oh." Apparently Lane and Bodhi have been moving much slower than Willa realized. Bodhi is sweet and laid-back and patient, but she's also easily distracted and pretty much into Hunter, for now anyway. Willa hates to think that Lane is waiting for Bodhi to make some major move that may never happen. "Well, sometimes you just have to put yourself out there. Don't overthink it. Take your moment when it comes, you know. Or it might never." The advice seems vague and useless even as she says it, but Willa has mixed feelings about helping Lane and Bodhi's relationship grow stronger—mixed as in, she doesn't want to, but feels bad about that.

Lane nods, then stands, brushing sand from her pants and hands. "Okay. We should get back then."

They take a path around the dunes and walk in silence back to the weathered dock. Willa thinks about what Lane said, about being authentic and about the years that she lost by not being honest with herself. Does Willa want to keep pushing her luck, waiting until the house of cards comes tumbling down and she has to start all over? Wait fourteen more years to figure out who she is, at Lane's age? But if she *becomes* the person she so badly wants to be, by winning this race, by carefully framing and filtering her life, then she never has to worry about that.

Lane unties the boat and readies the sails, letting Willa relax as she takes over the journey home. Once on a steady course though the sound, Lane tucks herself next to Willa. The sun is orange and low in the sky, and Willa turns to Lane to tell her that it's beautiful but she's not going to take a picture, just enjoy the moment—*see, she's not addicted to social media at all*—but Lane twists her torso and leans close.

She licks her lips, glances at Willa's mouth, and says, husky and breathless and shaking, "Can I kiss you?"

CH. *19*

HER HEART IN HER THROAT, lips parted in surprise, Willow can only stare in shock. Lane's dark eyes are hopeful; her face is already tipped close. Willow has to summon the strength of every bullshit lie she's ever told, every fabrication, every embellishment, in order to shake her head and say, "I don't think that's a good idea." She does. Oh, how she does.

Lane takes in a shocked little breath. "Oh. Okay." She moves away, though *away* in the tiny boat is a matter of inches. Lane's face shifts from disappointment to indifference. "Yeah. I don't know what I was..." She flicks her head, as if shaking the very idea of kissing Willa off and away.

"It's not that I don't want to," Willa blurts before she can stop herself. *God*, does she want to. "It's just, Bodhi..." If Lane is hung up on Bodhi, waiting for Bodhi to validate her attraction to women, then wanting to kiss Willa can only be because she's there and Bodhi isn't. It wouldn't even be Bodhi's sloppy seconds; it's Willa as a consolation prize. Worse than that even, she's a participation certificate, no meaning or connection, just a way for Lane to say she finally did it.

"Right, yeah. Bodhi."

After that, everything in Lane goes cold: her body language, her eyes, her voice, the way her back is turned to Willa for the rest of the trip home. The sun has set when they make it back to Lane's condo, and, though she must be as hungry and exhausted as Willa, Lane leaves almost immediately with a gym bag slung over one shoulder. There's no gym on Porter Island, just a yoga studio that shares space with a massage parlor that's sometimes an acupuncturist, which must be where Lane went. Willa could go after her. She doesn't.

For dinner, Willa eats some of the granola bars she stashed in her backpack, showers quickly, and checks her Instagram while the apartment grows dark around her. At least her horse photo got tons of likes and comments. She even got some new followers. At least online she isn't a disappointment, just a fraud.

She must have fallen asleep, because when she shifts and stretches on the couch, turning toward the glass sliding door, the full moon is suspended over the ocean outside. She checks her phone: 10:30. Lane's gym bag is dropped by the door, and, after a visit to the bathroom, Willa wanders sleepily to the closed bedroom door, where the sliver of space below it is pitch black. She hesitates there, though she isn't sure why. To apologize? Explain? Whatever the reason, she can't seem to move away; her heart is pumping too hard and making heat pool in her stomach and warm her face.

How long is she going to keep denying herself, keep ignoring the fact that she's desperately wanted Lane since the moment she saw her? And now Lane wants her back, and so what if it's only because Willa is a convenient stand-in for who Lane really wants? *Because,* Willa thinks weakly, because Bodhi is her friend and Bodhi likes Lane and Bodhi gets everything and Willa gets *nothing* and just this once can't she have something? Just this once, even if it's not really real, because nothing in Willa's life is really real and—

A light flicks on behind the door, just the soft glow of a nightlight or desk lamp shining a strip of faint gold on the carpet in front of Willa's bare feet. It's a signal or a sign or just an excuse to do what she was trying and failing to talk herself out of doing. She knocks on the door. Nothing. Then there's a swish of blankets, the creak of a bed frame, the snick of the doorknob.

"Wha— What are you—"

"I changed my mind," Willa says, then leans forward and presses her lips to Lane's mouth, still open in mid-question.

Lane sucks in a shocked breath, then takes control of the kiss, pushing her mouth firmly against Willa's and cupping her jaw. Willa doesn't get a chance to do more than flail her arms at her side before Lane pulls away. Her lips are still pursed, her palms are still around Willa's jaw, her eyes are dark.

Lane blinks, soft and slow. "Oh," she says. Then her eyebrows furrow, and she drops her hands. Willa immediately misses their warmth on her skin. "What about Bodhi?"

Irritation flushes through Willa, cooling the fire in her belly. She's so close to finally having this, she no longer cares about prioritizing Bodhi and what she might or might not want anymore. "Bodhi is out in the woods having sticky outdoor sex with someone else." Confusion crosses Lane's face, and she takes a step back. "Look, she doesn't really do committed relationships, I'm sorry."

"Why are you so—" Lane starts.

Willa is too wound up, too determined to do this and not think about it to talk about this right now, so she interrupts, "Bodhi isn't here, but I am and I—" Might as well be honest, she thinks, and moves closer, backing Lane into the end of the bed. "I really want this, okay? Bodhi will be still be there. I just want—" It sounds too much like begging and, for a terrifying moment, Willa is sure she's acted too rashly once again and screwed everything up. Maybe it was just a kiss, just to see. Maybe Lane didn't like kissing Willa after all, and now Willa looks desperate and pathetic. She looks down, voice barely over a whisper, "Do you… want this?"

Instead of answering, Lane kisses her again. Willa doesn't care that Lane would rather be kissing Bodhi and that this doesn't mean what Willa wants it to mean. Heat flares through her. Her body winds into Lane, and all she cares about are Lane's lips sliding and moving against hers, Lane's hands on her face and neck and shoulders and down to her hips, her palms sliding up Lane's back, the muscles there tensing and shifting beneath Willa's fingers. She can't care about anything but tumbling down onto the bed, slotting her legs between Lane's legs and her hands under Lane's shirt while Lane wriggles and pants beneath her. Maybe tomorrow she'll care about how much it will hurt to pretend that she isn't falling for Lane while Lane falls for someone else, but right now she doesn't care. She can't.

Willa focuses on kissing Lane, capturing her soft lips again and again, slipping her tongue into the damp heat of her mouth. She presses a kiss to Lane's neck, up behind her ear, and back to her mouth again, over and over until Lane is moaning and breathless. Willa isn't sure how much is too much and too fast, so she skims her fingertips across Lane's stomach, over the hard ridge of her hipbones and across the soft curve below her belly button, drags them slowly up between her ribs and lets her knuckles tease along the underside of her breasts. It feels like hours of this, of Willa building and building and building, keeping them both hovering on the precipice of more for *ages* until Lane huffs, grabs Willa's wrist, and shoves her hand into her pajama shorts.

"Oh, are you—" Willa swallows hard; her fingers flex toward that enticing heat. "Are you sure, because it's okay—"

"Christ, Willa, I'm not an untouched virgin. Get on with it."

If Willa had any notion that Lane in bed would somehow turn subdued and hesitant, she was clearly wrong. "Okay then," Willa says, unable to keep the amusement out of her voice. She pushes up onto one arm, shifts to the side a bit, and rests her hand on Lane's stomach instead of inside her pants. "I just thought you might be nervous. You know, your first girl-on-girl action and all."

Lane huffs again and mutters something that sounds like *oh my god* under her breath. She tugs Willa's shirt to bring her closer again, shoves Willa down onto her back and leans over, close, closer. "I'm just gonna..." Lane says, then pulls Willa's shirt up and off. Her eyes roam Willa's chest her hands tremble as she thumbs over Willa's nipples. "Sorry if I'm bad at this," Lane says, biting her lip then licking across it. She ducks her head so her warm breath raises goosebumps on Willa's skin. Willa's nipples stiffen, and she arches her back in anticipation, but instead of touching or kissing her breasts, Lane moves down. And down some more.

"Oh, right to it, okay," Willa mumbles, making room for Lane between her legs.

"Is that not— Should I do something else first?" Lane looks so serious, so determined, with eyebrows furrowed, mouth turned down, eyes on Willa's crotch as if she's found a particularly challenging puzzle there. But Willa isn't a problem to be solved.

"Yes," Willa says, body flushing not with just heat and desire but with adoration. "You should come back up here and kiss me."

CH. *20*

LANE DOESN'T COME BACK UP to kiss her, but does flop beside Willa with a dejected sigh. "I am bad at this," she says. "I'm not usually bad at things."

Willa turns to her side. Lane is lovely in profile: pillowy lips and lush, dark lashes and sharp, sloping jaw. "That's okay; practice makes perfect right?" She reaches for Lane, for the enticing strip of skin revealed below the hem of her twisted T-shirt. Lane sits up before she gets the chance.

"Not just— Not this." She gestures between them. "At admitting that I—" She pushes her hair back and sighs. "I didn't let myself think about this for so long and now that I can, it just feels *huge*, and I can't stop thinking about it and now here I am, fumbling around with no clue what I'm doing, and it's not as if I can train for this sort of thing or—"

"Hey," Willa interrupts, before Lane really works herself into a panic. "Maybe you're overthinking it."

"*Obviously* I'm overthinking it," Lane snaps. Then frowns. "Sorry."

Willa just knows somehow that Lane is the sort of person who rehearses phone calls before she makes them and practiced kissing on her own elbow and packs a suitcase two weeks before a trip and would never in a million years strap on a pair of roller skates and hope for the best or sign up for a sailing race with no actual knowledge of sailing. When Lane said her whole life was focused on sailing—training, preparing, winning—she must have meant that literally. Luckily for

Lane, Willa is the sort of person who throws herself into new situations with wild abandonment.

"So then, this can just be practice," Willa says, ignoring the voice in her head that pops up in dispute. Lane nods, relieved, until Willa adds, "It means nothing, okay?"

Lane's face snaps through a reaction, crumples for just a breath of a moment before turning flat and cold. "You know what? Actually, I'm really tired. I have be up early tomorrow."

The next thing Willa knows, she's looking at the closed door of Lane's bedroom, blinking in confusion. It could have all been a dream, a sleepwalking fantasy she had in the dark hallway of Lane's condo, if not for the shirt balled in her hands and the ache between her legs and the taste of Lane's skin still on her lips. *Did I say something wrong?* Willa tries to get comfortable on the couch and stares up at the ceiling as she plays through everything that just happened. Lane must have been uncomfortable about being inexperienced and talked herself out of it. She must have, because when Willow thinks, with hope, with yearning desire, that maybe Lane wants being with Willa to mean something, Willa has to stop those thoughts in their tracks.

Lane doesn't think of Willa that way. Lane likes Bodhi. Willa saw the way she looks at Bodhi, plus the fact that she brings her up constantly. No. She just got too nervous, and Willa needs to back off. Willa touches her lips and closes her eyes and falls asleep with a hollowness in her chest. In the morning, Lane is gone, and Willa's neck hurts from sleeping in a weird position. She packs her things and sets off for work, sleep-deprived and sad, telling herself over and over that Lane got cold feet. It's fine, it's not a big deal. Eventually she'll believe it.

"Hey, Wills! Where've you been?"

Willa glares at Bodhi, who looks even more tan and glowing than usual. "Where've I been? Where have you been?" She dumps her backpack and sleeping bag in the cramped corner in the back of the store that they call a break room. Her back hurts now after hauling all her stuff on the long walk to work. "You left me high and dry with nowhere to stay while you dicked around in the woods." More like left her wet and soggy, but still. "Some friend you are."

Bodhi chuckles. "Wow you woke up in a mood. All right."

"No, it's not all right." Willa wheels around, a small part of her protesting that she's angry at Bodhi over something that isn't her fault, but she can't seem to stop herself now that she's started. "You're so fucking self-centered Bodhi, and I'm sick of it."

Hurt creeps across Bodhi's placid face; her eyebrows furrow, and one arm crosses her chest. "I offered to have you stay with us."

"Yeah, as an afterthought, as a third wheel. Like I wanted to watch you and Hunter make out all weekend. And what even is that? You and Hunter? Just getting what you want, and who cares how she feels? You know she actually likes you, right? Like you care."

Once, not long after they met, Willa was at a party with Bodhi. A guy kept bothering this girl who was visiting for the summer, Willa can't remember her name now, but she kept trying to nicely put this guy off, asking him to stop, laughing off his refusal to take no for answer. They were refilling their cups at the keg, she and Bodhi and this girl, and the creep came over and grabbed the girl, just full on assaulting her, and Bodhi, quiet, chill, non-confrontational Bodhi, lost it. She just snapped, yelled at the guy, cursed him out, very nearly decked him before he went simpering away. It was the first and last time Willa saw Bodhi get angry. Until now.

"I don't know what the fuck your problem is," Bodhi says, moving into Willa's space aggressively. "But I suggest that you take your attitude and shove it, or I—"

"Girls!" They both startle and find Jenn walking toward them with a very disappointed look on her face. "What is going on back here?"

"Nothing," Bodhi says, stepping back.

"It's fine," Willa says, smoothing her shirt with shaking hands.

Jenn's arms cross. "Well, I don't believe you, but we have customers, so we can talk about this later." When they protest, Jenn gives them both a look that silences them immediately, then points to the front of the store. "Go."

"Yes, Mom." Bodhi mumbles.

"Yes, ma'am," Willa says.

Even though the store stays busy all day, it's the longest eight hours of Willa's life. Every time there's a slight lag in customers, she catches Bodhi looking at her, not with anger, which she would prefer, but with hurt. Willa is the worst friend of all time and she desperately wants to apologize and nearly does so several times. The thing is, if Willa confessed that she had feelings for Lane, she knows that Bodhi would back off. That's the kind of non-self-centered person Bodhi is. But she can't tell Bodhi that she was wrong, she can't be honest, because then Bodhi will know the sort of person that *Willa* really is. And then she'll really lose her.

Once the store is closed, Willa tries to avoid Jenn and Bodhi, pretending to clean something behind a back shelf while Bodhi cashes out. Only when it's quiet does Willa creep to cash out her own drawer in the back office. Where Bodhi still sits.

"Hey."

"Oh." Willa sets the drawer down. "Hey."

"I'm sorry if I made you feel unwelcome. I didn't realize." Bodhi looks up at her with those emerald eyes, so sincere, so apologetic. Willa feels even worse.

"Okay," Willa croaks. She sits down to count out the cash in her drawer.

"And you're more than welcome to stay at Hunter's place tonight. No making out, I promise." She grins and bumps Willa's knee with her own.

Willa is the *worst person in the whole world*. "Okay. Thanks."

"Cool. I'll wait for you." Bodhi stands, then leans against the wall with her hands in her pockets. The serene look is back on her freckled face. "Hey, you all right?"

"Mmhmm," Willa says, counting twenties and trying very hard not to cry. "Fine." Everything is fine. Nothing is fine.

CH. *21*

YOUR FOLLOWERS HAVEN'T HEARD FROM you in a while! Instagram tells her. *Make a new post and let everyone know what you're up to!*

Willa sends the rest of her spring break in exile at Hunter's place. True to her word, Hunter and Bodhi don't make out even once—at least, not in front of Willa. Still, there's a tenderness between them, an intimacy. It's clear in the way their eyes meet, in how Bodhi's hand lingers on Hunter's back when she passes, as though she can't help but touch. There's a magnetic pull that Willa can feel, as if she's stuck between them like a piece of scrap metal that's just getting in the way. She avoids them as much as possible.

Willa spots Lane twice: once at sunrise, when Willa stumbles to Hunter's kitchen in search of something to drink and stares blankly at the early morning low tide as she chugs a can of vaguely-lime-flavored carbonated water. Down the beach someone is doing yoga in the wet sand at the tidal line, and Willa knows it's Lane from the way she moves, from the tilt of her chin, from her dark hair shining in the soft sunlight. Unable to drink another sip, Willa goes back to sleep. She sees Lane two days later in the complex's parking lot, coming home in the evening, and Willa considers calling out to her. But what would she say? "Sorry things got awkward when we tried to sleep together?" No. So Willa ducks against a car until Lane is inside.

When the race is only days away, Willa finally takes off the time that Robin and Jenn gave her to practice sailing. Still afraid and unsteady, she nevertheless manages to skim up and down the island, back and forth, never far from shore. Sometime around her tenth trip, Willa realizes she's developed something of an instinct. Instead of talking herself through every tiny step and every shift of the wind, she finds herself adjusting the sails and moving the rudder without thinking, as if she can finally speak the language of the waves.

When race day arrives, Willa is not as terrified as she should be.

She wakes early, eats a high-protein breakfast in Hunter's kitchen that looks like Lane's kitchen, and watches the ocean rise and fall. Bodhi and Hunter don't wake while Willa dresses in the gear Lane gave her and ties her hair back. The waterproof pants and windbreaker swish loudly in the quiet condo as she gathers her stuff and goes outside to wait for Robin and Jenn. They'll take her to the starting point, where Mr. Kelley will be waiting with the boat.

"Should be a beautiful day for it," Jenn says, after picking Willa up, as she drives north to the longest stretch of public beach access on the island.

"Should be a fun one," Robin adds, twisting in the passenger seat to give Willa's knee an encouraging pat.

It reminds Willa of her own mom, chattering fake-happily about the sunshine as Willa prepared to trudge off to another miserable, lonely day at school. "Have fun and be yourself!" she'd say, as if Willa would do either.

The parking lot and beach are crowded, and some boats are collecting in the water at the starting area, which is marked by orange buoys.

They find Mr. Kelley at the launch area. "Where's your coach?" he asks.

"Oh, she's—" Willa waves a hand vaguely in the direction of the crowd on the beach, though she's certain that Lane isn't there. "Great day for it, huh?" she says, successfully distracting Mr. Kelley with talk of the wind and wave conditions.

Willa checks in and learns that she'll be one of the last to launch, and it seems as if the whole morning passes as she waits for the other boats to gather in a clutch at the starting gate. Then, finally, it's almost her turn. She quickly takes and uploads a few pictures and short videos of the event, tightens her life vest, and rubs sunscreen on her face and neck. Robin and Jenn wish her luck and tell her that they're so proud of her, and Willa stammers and blushes and takes a deep breath before boarding her skiff.

"Willa! Willa, over here!"

One foot lifted off the dock, Willa looks up. "Mom?"

If not for the spray of water hitting her face and the heat of the sun on her skin, Willa would swear she was still asleep and dreaming. There, on a patch of sand near the launch site are her mom and her mom's husband and their two little kids, waving and smiling and calling her name. Willa stares, then jumps when a horn blares. She waves back and takes the signal to get in her boat and into position. The shock of seeing her mom makes Willa fumble with the lines and get a shaky start as she heads out into the water. Robin and Jenn go to talk with Willa's mom. Willa's foot gets tangled in a rope.

Once out on the water, Willa tries to stay in the back and away from the collection of boats drifting around the starting gate. She's not used to maneuvering around so many boats so close together and makes a note to give everyone a wide berth during the race. Seagulls scream nearby. The wind pushes the sails in and out. A racing official dressed in red zips past in a red motorboat.

What's Mom doing here? How did she find out? Willa finally gets her foot free from the rope and tries to focus on the race and only the race. Then she wonders, with a heavy sinking in her gut, what her mom is talking about with Robin and Jenn. It's not a stretch to think that her mom would mention that Willa has never competed in a sailing race, that she's never sailed before, ever, at all. It occurs to Willa that while she's bobbing on the water the whole house of cards she has built as her fake life is crashing down.

94

She's so distracted that when the first horn blares, warning everyone that the race is about to begin, Willa thinks it's the starting signal and jumps the gun, releasing the mainline and luffing out the sail, catching a gust of wind that sends her lurching ahead, and right into the hull of another boat.

A whistle blows. The referee boat hoists a black flag. Willa doesn't need her years of theoretical sailboat racing knowledge to know that's bad.

She's ejected from the race.

Disqualified. Hit with violating Rule 12 from the official Racing Rules of Sailing: *A boat clear astern shall keep clear of a boat clear ahead* and Rule 14: *A boat shall avoid contact with another boat if reasonably possible.*

And that's it. She's finished before she even started, disqualified before the race even began. The starting signal sounds, and the boats take off while Willa docks and drags herself, dejected, back to the beach. Bodhi has joined the crowd who gathered to watch her fail. No, she didn't fail; she didn't even *start*. How did it end like this? All that preparation, the worries, the scheming, the lies, for what? Her mom and her mom's husband and their kids and Robin and Jenn and Bodhi all gather around her; their faces are etched with confusion and pity. And, if the pitying looks from these two families, who are there for each other no matter what while Willa has herself and no one else, weren't bad enough, it gets even worse. After generic words of sympathy from everyone, it's Bodhi who says what everyone seems to be thinking.

"Willa, why in the world would you enter a sailing race if you've never sailed before?"

CH. *22*

WILLA FALTERS, GLANCING BACK AND forth at the group gathered around her, unsure which lie to tell. If she says that of course she's sailed before, she's just rusty still is all, her mom will know that's untrue. She could say that she's been sailing a lot in the years since her mom moved away and started a new life without her, though of course Jenn, Robin, and Bodhi will know that's not true. The wind gusts around them, and in the distance the flock of sailboats glides across the water, the race going on without her, their sails high and colorful in the bright blue sky. Down the beach, Willa spots Lane, and her heart soars. Lane came to see her! Oh, but Lane saw her ruin everything before it even began. But she could escape, say she needs to talk to her coach and put off this whole disaster, perhaps forever if she disappears into the crowd and keeps going. But she can't deal with how she's disappointing Lane, too, how everything she did for Willa was a waste of time, so Willa looks away.

It's the end. The end of everything.

As everyone stands around waiting for Willa to explain, and Willa waits for everyone to turn on her, her little brother Atticus whines, squirming and dancing, "I hafta go potty." Willa's mom looks around, toward where the public bathrooms used to be, but they tore the old ones down a few years ago and put in new ones with water-saving toilets and automatic sinks several yards farther up the shore.

"I'll take him!" Willa blurts. "I— I know where the bathrooms are." She grabs his hand before anyone can protest.

On the trek up, Atticus holds tight to Willa's hand, completely trusting that Willa has his best interest in mind. He manages to kick up more sand than a windstorm, takes the wooden stairs one painstaking step at a time, and clutches himself in a way only a three-year-old can get away with.

"You don't need help or anything, do you?" Willa asks, holding the stall door closed, since Atticus seems to have no qualms about leaving it wide open while he does his business.

"No!"

Thank god. While she waits, Willa tries to form a plan. She can send Atticus back down the beach by himself and she can take off. Go to Hunter's house and get her stuff, then take the ferry to the mainland. She has enough money for bus fare to get to— Where, exactly? And what if Bodhi goes back to Hunter's place before Willa leaves? If she rides her bike, she'll be much faster than Willa will be on foot.

"My pants are stuck!" Atticus calls, and Willa sighs. What chance does this child have of making it back to his parents on a crowded beach if he can't figure out his own pants?

Resigned to her fate, Willa sighs. "Okay, I'll help you."

She takes her time, going even slower than a three-year-old's pace allows. She and Atticus stop to watch a predatory cluster of seagulls close in on a teenager with a bag of chips. Atticus chases the birds down the beach until they disperse and fly away, then Willa chases him, and then they watch the sailboats now far off, like toy boats bobbing on the waves.

"Well, time to face the guillotine," she says, holding out her hand.

"Huh?" He takes her hand and looks up at her for an answer. Atticus and their two-year-old sister Amelia are perhaps the only people she hasn't completely betrayed and misled, who have any reason to still trust her, and that's only because they barely know her.

"Nothing," Willa says. Time to finally come clean.

Back by the shoreline only her mom and her mom's husband, with little Amelia tucked in his arms, are still there. Her mom gives Willa a very familiar look when they approach, one of disappointment.

"Mom." Willa's voice cracks. Atticus lets go of her hand to dig a hole into the sand with only his little hands.

"We will talk about it later," her mom says, definitively. "Now then, we're only in town for the weekend, so why you don't come with us to our hotel room. We'd like to spend some time with you." Her mom's husband looks dubious. Willa feels the same way. But what choice does she have? Where else can she go?

"Yeah, okay."

* * *

THEY HAVE LUNCH AT HER mom's favorite seafood restaurant, where the fish comes battered and deep fried, with a side of coleslaw and hush puppies that leave blotches of grease on the paper-lined plastic baskets. They sit on a deck over the water, where Amelia and Atticus can run around and throw french fries to the seagulls that stalk the place.

"So what are you—" Tim, says. "Um. How are you... lately?"

Tim has graying black hair and a round, flat face. He's older than her mom by several years, divorced but with no other children. Willa has only seen him in pleated, pressed khakis and button-up shirts in various shades of blue, though admittedly she hasn't seen him very many times. Today's shirt is periwinkle, perhaps brighter than usual on account of his beach vacation.

"I'm not great, Tim," Willa quips, spearing a deep-fried shrimp. "Not great."

"Willa," her mom warns, in the same tone she just used to tell Amelia that she needed to stop licking other people's chairs.

"It's okay, Christina," Tim says. "Rather indecorous of me." He chuckles. Willa rolls her eyes at him. "I'm sure everything will blow over soon," he adds.

98

"I doubt it."

"Okay then," her mom says. "Let's talk about it. What exactly happened?"

Willa chews her shrimp, shakes her head, and mumbles, "I dunno."

Her mom considers this, clearly dissatisfied, but says, "Fine then, you can stay with us this weekend; I'll go to the house and pick some stuff up for you. You can take time to figure things out. And then we will talk." She glances at Tim, who seems to indicate that he's fine with this plan. "But Willa, you're better than this."

Willa nods. She's pretty sure she isn't.

Atticus and Amelia need a nap, so they all hunker down in the hotel room, which is outfitted with two double beds and a stiff upholstered chair. Tim lies down with the kids and nods off before they do; the three of them softly snore while Christina tidies up the toys and tiny little shoes littering the room. Willa sits sideways in the uncomfortable chair, with her phone in her hand but not turned on, trying to come up with some bullshit post about being disappointed but that true success means getting back up and how she can't wait to get back out there. *Ugh.*

Atticus snuffles and rolls over, curling up closer to Amelia. It's funny, Willa thinks, how she decided that they both look exactly like Tim, and because they are Tim's, that they're foreign to her. But Amelia's wispy brown hair is growing in the same spirals as her own, and their mom's, hair. Atticus's chin is dimpled, just like hers, just like their grandfather's. There's something about the way they both laugh, hiccupping and high-pitched, that is so familiar, so like her own. She's been reluctant to claim them, but now that the chips are down, who is there? Just this. Her family, which she supposes includes Tim, who is maybe not so bad and looks at her mom as if she's the best thing that's ever happened to him. Maybe living in Kansas City wouldn't be so bad.

After nap time, her mom and Tim take the kids to the beach, though the whole complicated procedure of getting the kids into bathing suits and sunscreen and hats, then packing a cooler and diaper bag and toy bag and chairs and umbrellas hardly seems worth it. Willa stays behind, claiming that she isn't up to it, and, in truth, she really isn't.

Once they finally leave, she gets onto Instagram, ready to go with a cheesy quote and a black-and-white picture of a dandelion growing through the sidewalk that she took some time ago. Her stomach sinks when she looks at her notifications. Someone got a video of the crash at the starting gate and tagged her in it. There's comment after comment about her poor sportsmanship and how it was an attempt at cheating, and others pointing out that she clearly didn't do it on purpose because she clearly didn't know what the hell she was doing. Those are worse. She's lost a good chunk of followers, including some of the companies that she does affiliate posts for. The number continues to plummet as she watches. Her planned post is suddenly insufficient. She doesn't know what to say, which comments to address first or at all, so she closes down the app, then shuts off her phone.

Kansas City may not be far enough.

CH. *23*

AMELIA AND ATTICUS GO TO bed at seven p.m. sharp, even on vacation. Willa's mom and Tim settle into the other bed and snuggle up to watch something on a laptop with one pair of earbuds stretched between them. Willa puts in her own earbuds and tries to find a comfortable position on the rollaway bed, which proves to be difficult because it seems that, instead of being stuffed with springs and cotton, it was filled with knives and sawdust. After she squeaks the wobbly metal frame one too many times, Christina shushes her, so Willa gives up on finding a comfortable position and accepts her miserable fate.

It's not even dark out, Willa laments, silently and to herself lest she be shushed again. She's on her stomach, draped partway off the bed with her phone on the floor and one arm dangling to scroll listlessly. Every time she checks her Insta, she's lost more followers. The veil concealing her true reality was even flimsier than she thought: one mistake, just one misstep, and that was it, gone. Her followers, her job, her relationship with Jenn and Robin, her friendship with Bodhi, half of her rent, all of her dignity, gone. Lacking the even the slightest bit of self-preservation, Willa checks on her follower account again, then sighs so loudly that she checks over her shoulder to make sure it didn't wake any small children. She clicks on her own profile and plays the last video she took.

"I just want to thank everyone real quick for all of their support," Willa says on the video, with the sun-dappled ocean behind her, her hair in wild tendrils, the sound of a sail snapping in the wind, the boat rocking on choppy little waves. "You have made me realize that I am stronger and braver and more capable than I ever thought possible. And if anyone out there is facing a difficult hurdle, I hope this inspires you to just go for it despite your fears. You have so much more to gain by trying and failing than never trying at all."

They're bullshit platitudes that meant nothing at all, but people ate it up all the same. Willa shuts her phone off and yanks out her earbuds. The only sounds in the room are the occasional gust of wind that's strong enough to rattle the shutters and Tim's weird, whistling nose breathing. Is this what she's resigned her life to? Tiptoeing around the sleeping schedule of toddlers and pretending she hasn't resented Tim for years because he took her mom away and pretending she didn't resent her mom more for going. Is she giving up her home, her friends, her life, the persona she's spent so much time and effort cultivating for *years* only to lie here in the dark on a shitty, fold-up hotel bed and let everything crumble? *No.*

She sits bolt upright. The bed screeches. Her mom shushes her. Tim's nose whistles. *I'm going out,* Willa mouths. Her mom's eyebrows lift, but she nods.

It's still light out and blustery when she reaches the marina. Her mom thought to retrieve her skateboard; it felt like being reunited with an old friend when she got it back in her arms—her only friend, now. Willa kicks the board up and sets it against a tree before making sure Mr. Kelley isn't in the marina office. She quietly makes her way down the dock to where the boat is usually tied up. But it's not there; the spot is empty. Is it still at the race launch site? One of the officials who reprimanded Willa did say something about an investigation. Willa glances around at the other boats docked on the slip. She could just take one and bring it right back; no one will miss it. What if someone does miss it, though, and she's arrested for stealing a boat? If only she knew of a boat that no one ever uses… At a house where no one ever seems to be home…

Willa makes herself to go as fast her muscles and the board will let her, pushing hard against the pavement and taking every shortcut she can think of. The sunlight fades; everything is dark blue and moody around her. The strong wind howls around her; that should help move things along. She'll be back before dark, no problem.

There are no lights on at the Cordova house. Willa takes the long, winding driveway slowly. No cars are in the garage when she peeks in; she sees no signs of life inside the house when she presses her face against the dark windows. "I'm just borrowing Lane's boat," Willa tells herself as she thunks down the walkway and winds through the wetlands. She'll follow the race course and redeem herself, complete the race as she knows she can, and everything will be fixed. She'll tell Robin and Jenn and Bodhi that she didn't tell her mom about the sailing and the shoulder injury, because her mom is afraid she'll get hurt again. That makes sense. And she would have worried too much. And she'll tell her mom, separately, that it was all a misunderstanding. It was her first boat race *ever*, but Robin and Jenn must have misheard and thought she'd been racing *forever*.

And as for her followers, Willa decides as she approaches the dock, she'll go live while she successfully runs this course, explain that a sudden rush of wind caught her off guard, that it happens! All the time! And she's for sure going to enter another race soon. She can fix this. She can right this ship. It's not too late.

Willa's pace slows and she stops. Lane's boat isn't here, just the larger daysailer with a below-deck cabin that's meant to be comfortable for weekend trips. It's much bigger and more complicated than what she's used to, but it'll sure look great on her video. Willa hops into the boat before she can change her mind and sets about figuring out all of the many unfamiliar lines and ropes and the complex navigation system. After she works out how to get the sails up, Willa starts a new video, holding her phone high as she loops the anchor rope free and the sun sets behind her. Far off in the distance, thunder rumbles. She needs to be quick.

"Hey, everyone, so earlier today was a definitely a disappointment. For me most of all. And I know for you all too. But I wanted to explain and encourage all of you out there that we aren't going to let a little setback make us give u—"

"What the hell are you doing?"

Willa screams, spins around, and fumbles her phone. She drops it right into the water with a sad little *plop* and loses her grip on the mainsail all in the same terrifying moment. "Lane! What are you doing here?"

Lane lifts her hands in an exasperated gesture. "I came to check on my parents' house because they're out of town and I heard talking— Why am I explaining myself? Why are *you* here?"

"Uh." Willa tries to buy herself some time. A curtesy boat check? Sleepwalking? The wind gusts, and the boat lurches forward. Willa stumbles and flails, then grabs blindly for whatever rope is nearest. "Well, I'm…"

"You're sailing away!" Lane says.

"Yes," Willa acknowledges. She is, it seems, doing just that. "But I swear I'll be right back. Just—" The boat sways to the side, bumping along the dock, out of control. Willa reaches out to push the boat away and out farther into the water, but only scrapes her palms on the dock. "Shit, ow. Super quick!"

"Willa, there's a storm coming tonight, and you don't know how to work a boat that big. You need to come back." Lane jogs down the dock until there's no dock left.

Willa watches Lane and the dock slip away behind her. The boat rapidly picks up speed as it ricochets out of the shallow water. *A storm. She doesn't know how.* The waves are so much bigger and more violent that Willa realized; the wind is so much stronger. Another roll of thunder rumbles nearby, and Willa feels seasick. She holds on to the sturdy mast in the center of the boat, closes her eyes, takes deep breaths, and tries to not puke. Okay, she just has to turn around. Just figure out which line releases the boom so she can figure out how to turn the boat. That's all. Only she can't seem to let go of the mast. Or open her eyes. *Oh, no.*

Then there's a loud thump, and a louder string of curse words, and Willa opens her eyes to find Lane sprawled on the deck.

CH. 24

LANE GROANS AND SITS UP. "I hurt my ankle." She rubs at her right ankle, then hisses.

"Oh, my god," Willa says. Lane must have launched herself from the edge of the dock; she's lucky if she only twisted her ankle a bit. "Why did you do that?"

"You froze up! What was I supposed to do?" Lane tries to stand; she hisses and sits back down. "Plus, you were stealing my parents' boat."

"I was borrowing it!" Willow protests, but her indignation doesn't last long. The boat rocks dangerously after a huge gust of wind and then slams into a wave. Willa collapses next to Lane, and is suddenly so, so grateful that Lane stupidly launched herself into the moving boat. In a small, trembling voice, Willa asks, "What do we do now?"

Lane watches the way the sails catch the wind, then scans the shore. They aren't too far out, though the boat has begun to make it around and out of the sound and is heading toward the open ocean. They aren't too far from where the race course began, and, with the wind and Lane's know-how, it shouldn't take Willa long at all. She's come this far.

"It's not too late to head back," Lane says, straining to reach for a rope. "I just need a little help."

"No!" Willa knocks the rope away. "I can't go back."

"Willa, what is wrong with—"

"I can't. Please." Willa hates the way Lane is looking at her, as though she's some out of control child and she hates even more that she feels like one. "I've lost everything. My job and my friends and my reputation and my... followers," she adds the last one weakly, sheepish, but that meant something to her. All those people who saw the person that she wanted to be mattered to her. Of course, now that she's dropped her phone into the ocean, this whole redemption cruise will be a harder sell. It's not just for the followers though; it's so Willa knows that she can still be that person at least one more time before she has to leave it all behind. "This is all I have, Lane. I need to do this. I need a win. I know you understand what that's like."

Lane frowns. Her eyes dart from Willa to the turbulent sails to the black clouds. "Oh, god. Okay." She shakes her head. "This is so reckless, but okay." She scoots toward the back of the boat. "I'll take the rudder; you follow my instructions."

They get the boat on course; the two of them work in perfect tandem to steer it on the choppy waves, carefully adjusting the sails to the whipping wind. The storm descends in increments, slowly consuming them instead of hitting all at once: It grows dark first, darker than dusk, then darker than nightfall. The hairs on Willa's arm stand on end from the crackling electricity. The boat itself groans and creaks, protesting the storm. At the rudder, Lane uses all of her strength to push and pull. She shoves her shoulder into the handle and braces herself with her good foot. The mast bends against Willa's efforts to hold the sails steady; the ropes are pulled so tight they cut into her hands. Waves curl over the side of the boat and splash across Willa's feet. Her sneakers slip and slide as if the deck is made of ice. But they're close, so close. Lightning slithers across the sky, and thunder claps a low, angry roar. Willa shivers, sets her teeth, and stands her ground. Then one of the sails rips.

"Damn," Lane says. "We need to take in the sails."

"What?" Willa glances back. Lane is pale faced; her hair sticks in sweaty clumps to her face. Willa realizes that Lane's exhausted as well. "We're almost there! We have to keep going!"

"If we keep going, we won't have a boat left to make it there!" Lane yells. "Take in the sails, Willa!"

Willa hesitates, torn between her own need to finish this no matter how dangerous and the reality that Lane is right and they're in danger of losing the sails altogether, maybe even snapping the mast or rudder. Fighting the wind and water and her own reckless instincts, Willa releases the tension on the line she's holding and frees the sail.

Lane tries to help as much as she can, but Willa has to haul in the lines, drop the sails, and lock the tiller to leeward. Then, nearly spent, she helps Lane hobble across the slick deck and down the stairs to the small cabin space.

"So, we're just drifting now?" Willa says, panting and weak in the entryway of the cabin. The cabin is no bigger than a walk-in closet with much less headroom. A U-shaped sitting area takes up most of the floor space, and there's a tiny kitchenette and tinier bathroom. Its shining caramel-colored wood and white leather accents give it a certain elegance. And, unlike the Cordova's home, it's filled with personal items. A fishing hat is nestled into the small shelf that runs above the seats; a floppy white sunhat is tucked companionably next to it. There are well-loved books and a stack of board games, a pair of binoculars and a canister of fancy herbal tea. There's even a picture of Lane's whole family: her parents and brother and a younger Lane smiling on the deck of this same boat. Her family seems to be happy only when they're gone; it must have been so hard for Lane to give that up and stay in one place.

"That was when they first got it," Lane says. "Our first trip out." She ducks, carefully makes her way to the edge of a cushion, and drops down with an obvious wince. "There's water and towels in the floor compartment; grab me one of each." She nods at a handle tucked flat into the floorboards; it's a cabinet that's hidden below the seating area. There's food, too, Willa discovers as she curiously opens and closes all the little hidden nooks and crannies to find just dry goods and some jugs of water. "And no," Lane says, finally answering Willa's question.

"Since we lashed the helm in place, the bow will be kept to windward of the beam. It should hold us steady."

Willa collects two bottles of water and hands one to Lane. Then she opens the bathroom closet and realizes it's not big enough to change in and there isn't anywhere to strip off her damp clothes in private.

"I need to—" Lane plucks at her soaked shirt.

Despite being on a boat getting tossed around at sea during a storm with no one at the helm, Willa's most pressing concern is the awkwardness of the situation and the memory of the last time they were nearly naked in front of each other.

"I'll just—" Willa turns away, coming nose-to-nose with the wall and hunched over like an old witch in a kids' movie. She waits until Lane gives the okay, then tugs off her wet shirt. She sits on the other side of the U in her board shorts and bathing suit top.

Lane, wearing less beneath her towel, stretches out, propping her injured ankle on a seat back. Too much of her bare leg shows when the towel slips off her strong thigh. Willa has to look away. "It's swollen," she says, eyes fixed on Lane's ankle.

"Yeah. Hurts too."

The boat rocks and sways, waves slap the side, thunder and lightning chase each other in a rapid series of flashes and booms.

"Now what?"

"You keep saying that," Lane replies.

"Well, you're the one who knows what they're doing here."

Lane leans back on her elbow; more of the towel slips off her thigh. "I don't sail in storms. Never took the chance. I couldn't have done that without you. I *wouldn't* have done that without you." She takes an audible breath and looks at Willa with dark, serious eyes. "So, Willa. Now what?"

CH. 25

LANE LOOKS AT HER EXPECTANTLY, as if Willa has any idea of what to do. The boat rocks hard enough that some books and the binoculars fall to the floor.

"Are we in like, immediate danger?" Willa says, with a nervous glance at a porthole window. Lane makes a noise that Willa does not find reassuring. Willa really screwed up here. Again. It wasn't bad enough that she's put herself at risk, stole a boat, and lost her phone. She's put Lane in danger too. "I'm sorry," Willa says, not sure what she should apologize for first. "I can't get anything right. I'm such a fuck-up, I'm sorry."

With some effort, Lane sits up. "Willa, we're gonna be fine."

Willa shakes her head; tears cloud her vision. "I'm not."

Lane is quiet, then says, "My parents always keep a bottle of wine here. Check in that skinny cabinet next to the stove. Corkscrew should be in the drawer above."

Willa gives her a quizzical look, then does what Lane instructed, finding a bottle of red wine that has a label written entirely in Italian and is probably very expensive. "Is now really the time?" Willa wonders, handing everything over to Lane.

"If there was ever a time for wine, this is it."

They skip the glasses, instead passing the bottle back and forth. It's bitter and harsh to Willa's untrained palate—when she drinks it's usually tequila shots or cheap beer or something pink and fruity—but after a few swallows the wine becomes warm and velvety on her tongue.

"Better?" Lane's eyes are bright when she takes the bottle back; her cheeks and lips are flushed. Willa notices that her hair, usually so perfectly straight and styled without a strand out of place, is drying in messy, fluffy waves. It makes her look sweeter, Willa thinks, softer at the edges.

"Better," Willa says.

"My last race," Lane starts, taking a swig of wine, then setting the bottle between her bare knees, "I knew I had to go out with a bang. Nothing but first place was good enough, not like it ever was, but. I trained my ass off. It was like, if I could just get that one last big win, then giving it all up would be fine. My parents had been pressuring me to join my brother at their office here and start doing these showy yacht club regattas instead of comps. But it didn't matter that it was the last thing I wanted, because I was going out on top and they'd be proud of me. That's what I told myself anyway."

"And you did," Willa guesses. "Of course you did." Lane is amazing and actually has her life together and is not a complete disaster of a human like Willa.

Lane passes the wine back. "You feel as if no one will love you for you, only for what you can do or what you can offer them, right? With my family, hell everyone I've been close to, that's exactly how it was. As long as I was sailing and winning races I could justify giving up all these pieces of myself."

Willa sips the wine, wipes her mouth, and says, "Yeah. That's crap though. I mean, if they don't love you for you, then they don't deserve to be in your life. Cuz you're awesome." Lane lifts an eyebrow.

"Oh," Willa says. That's the whole thing, isn't it? The boat lurches dangerously, and Willa has to grab for the wine as it pitches toward the floor.

Lane tips her head in acknowledgement. "Anyway, my last race. After hovering in the middle of the pack for a while, I got a break and started to pull ahead. Third place, then second. I pushed myself to the absolute limit, way past what I should have, but I could *taste* it, you know?" Willa offers her the wine bottle, but she doesn't take it. She's too busy gesturing and leaning close to tell the story; she has a distant look in her eyes as if she's right back there in the action, so close to victory and, perhaps, to proving her own worth to everyone who has convinced her that she doesn't have it.

"So finally, on the last leg, I'm gaining on the first place position. I cut left, close, helm to stern. But that's as close as I can get, no matter what I do. Now, you're supposed to give a warning when you pass that closely. That's a hard rule because it's a safety issue. But they hadn't noticed me, and I thought: I need an advantage. I justified it by telling myself that I had no choice. So I cut closer and decided to not to alert them. And—" She hits the palm of one hand against the fingers of the other. "They shifted port just a little, and we collided. Their boat was okay, but I was disqualified. That was the end for me."

Willa's head is swimming from the wine and the way the boat is swaying and a little bit from the way Lane leaned close while telling her story. The towel fell loose from her shoulders as she grew more and more animated.

"Just like—" Willa says.

"Just like you. Only I knew better." Lane, noticing how low her towel has fallen, blushes and shrugs it up higher. "You're not a screw-up. After that race, after being forced to come crawling back to my parents to a job I never wanted, I stopped trying. But, god, you try so hard, Willa. Please never be ashamed of that."

The boat sways, or maybe it's just Willa, and she finds herself listing forward, holding on to Lane's shoulders to keep herself steady. Moving in just a breath more to kiss Lane, soft and slow, seems like the most natural, the most right thing she's ever done.

Willa moves away to catch her breath, far enough to check with Lane and make sure that was okay, though the way Lane responded, with hands immediately cupping Willa's jaw and mouth moving against hers and the high, wanting whine she gave when Willa pulled away seemed to be an enthusiastic *yes*. But still. Things have been weird between them, and Lane sort of panicked on her last time they tried this, so better be sure.

"Are you—" Lane's eyes are still closed; her face is lifted and mouth slightly pursed. It makes Willa chuckle. "Um. Are you sure…"

Lane's eyes pop open, and irritation crosses her face. It's a look Willa has believed to be her fault for being an idiot, but it seems to just be the way Lane is wired with a filter-free expression of emotions rather than Willa's approach, which is to pretend everything is fine even as it all crashes down around her.

Lane shakes her head, as if to clear it. "You're right, maybe I— I've had too much wine." She frowns, and Willa's heart sinks. She did it again, ruined the moment. Then Lane heaves a breath. "Look, I'm not totally comfortable with you and Bodhi's whole thing. But I can deal with it, if that's what you— Maybe I'm just old? Dating is so confusing nowadays."

Willa squints, fuzzy with the wine and the lingering effects of kissing Lane, and runs that over in her head a few times before it sinks in. "Me… and Bodhi? What… What thing?"

"You know the—" She waves a hand. "Open relationship? Polyamory? Is that the term you all prefer? It's just not my thing? No judgement! I looked it up. I'm fine with it. Or, I'm sort of not but—"

"Wait." Lane stops rambling. Willa focuses her thoughts. "Bodhi and I do not have any sort of relationship. Open or otherwise."

Lane's mouth parts in surprise. "Oh."

This is ridiculous. Lane couldn't have possibly thought— All this time— "I thought *you* were into Bodhi!" Giddiness mingles with confusion, and Willa almost laughs. It's not funny, not yet. "The way you were looking at her at the party, I thought…"

"Oh, that." Lane blushes. "You saw that. I mean, she's quite attractive? For so long I hadn't let myself look at attractive women without convincing myself that I wasn't looking. So maybe I…" She frowns. "Maybe I was being a little obvious."

Willa laughs, then Lane laughs. The situation is absurd, she thought Lane liked Bodhi and Lane thought she was with Bodhi, and if Bodhi was here she would think it was hilarious too. Well, if she didn't hate Willa for being a liar, she would. That thought is sobering enough for Willa to focus back on Lane. Does that mean then that Lane is actually into her?

"So," Willa says, moving back into Lane's space. "Have you been looking at *me*?"

Lane nibbles on her lip coyly. "As a matter of fact—"

Crack!

They both startle. Something happened above them on the deck; a lightning strike or something snapping off in the high wind.

"I'll go," Willa says, without a moment's hesitation, and climbs up, right into the storm.

"Willa, wait!"

 CH. *26*

THE MAST HAS BROKEN JUST as they worried it might; it snapped in two right under the top spreader. The upper portion is now flapping loose in the wind, banging against the intact bottom portion. The jib has fallen limp, leaving no mainsail to keep the boat on course. Without it they have nothing to hold them steady against the wind and waves, nothing to stop the storm from tossing them about aimlessly. She has to lower it, Willa realizes, then take control of the tiller and steer the boat with it and the smaller secondary sails as best as she can. Fighting against the wind and the violent waves, Willa pulls and pulls, rain blinding her, slipping and grunting, and manages to get the mainsail down and the secondary sails up.

Lightning cracks so close Willa can feel it snap through the air and she takes off across the deck, back to Lane and the safety of the cabin. She doesn't account for how slippery the deck is under her sneakers and how wildly the boat is tossing. A wave rears up, the wind pushes against her, and Willa loses her footing, falling like a cartoon character on a banana peel, legs flying out in front of her, the world going sideways. She hears Lane call her name, faint and faraway, just before she comes down hard.

Her head hurts and then it doesn't.

She can see the sky, patches of blue peeking out from heavy black clouds, and then she can't see anything.

Lane is there and then she's not.

When Willa opens her eyes, she's flat on her back, only she's somehow at the skating rink. She's seven. She's fallen, again, and all of her classmates are gathered around.

"I thought you were good," one of them says.

"Yeah, can you even skate?" another demands.

A disco ball twirls above her, and the skating rink DJ is spinning NSYNC. "Bye, bye, bye," Justin Timberlake croons, and Willa sits up. Her head is killing her.

"I can skate," she protests. Her voice sounds weird, grown-up.

"Yeah, right," says another classmate, and then they all skate away, the whole group huddled together like a pack of baby chicks. Willa is never part of that group and she's only now beginning to understand why.

When her mom picks her up in their old, ugly car, Willa, face burning, climbs into the back and doesn't answer her mom when she asks how it went.

"Just go," Willa says in her weird grown-up voice. She doesn't talk to her mom at all on the drive to the ferry, doesn't get out when her mom asks if she wants to come, even though that's her favorite part, standing at the rails on the upper deck and watching the ocean go by. When they get home, Willa goes right to her room, sits on her bed, and scowls down at her yard-sale dress and the hand-me-down shoes from her mom's co-worker's daughter, who is one year older than Willa, who got the shoes already used from her older sister.

Most of her classmates wear new clothes and shoes no one else has worn. They have shiny cars and huge houses and someone they call Nanny to take them places and pick them up after school. Willa walks home, by herself, and goes into her small house by herself. She doesn't know anyone called Nanny.

"What's wrong, baby?" Willa's mom asks again over dinner. It's mac and cheese in the little blue boxes, not the name brand but the store brand, which is Willa's favorite, and so she has never wondered why they have it so often.

"I can't skate," is all Willa can say when she wants to ask why she had to rent the ugly brown skates at the rink instead of bringing the ones with wheels all in a row that are neon pink and neon green and have buckles that make a cool sound when you tighten them. Why has she never gone skating like her classmates, who have gone "a million times," or so they say.

"You just have to try again, sweet pea." Her mom is in her cleaning uniform, the brown polyester shirt and pants, the ones that Willa will soon forbid her mom from wearing in public when they're together.

In middle school she has to take the ferry every morning to a town all the way across the sound, where she and her classmates become a handful of students in a population of hundreds. There are more people in her graduating class in high school than there are on her whole island. She can be someone else there and she is. Her parents own a chain of hotels, she tells people, a small one. It sounds more humble to say that, she thinks. Her dad works so hard and is gone so much, but he loves them a whole lot, oh, he just hates to be away, she insists. It's her most desperate wish, come to life as a lie. In high school, in a town where she doesn't live, Willa is cooler, smarter, better. This is the person Bodhi meets, who asks her if she likes to sail when they sit together on the ferry after school, who wonders if she needs a job, who led her here, adrift on the ocean in a storm.

If she had learned to roller skate, maybe none of that would have happened.

If she hadn't been ashamed of her mom, who worked so hard to put food on the table and gas in their crappy old car, maybe Willa would be a better person.

If she had just been honest—

If.

If...

She's back at the skating rink, in a grown-up body to match her grown-up voice. Her classmates aren't there, just her, in the center of the rink with spots of light swirling and swirling around her.

117

"We're so proud of you!" calls a voice from the crowd. It's Jenn, standing outside the rink on the carnival-bright carpet.

"You can win this!" adds Robin.

There are other skaters now, but they're in boats. It seems like an unfair advantage.

"I can't." She tries to explain. She doesn't know how to roller skate; she doesn't have a boat; she doesn't even know how she got here.

"Can you even sail?" Asks Bodhi, who is standing next to Willa's mom, who is wearing her brown polyester cleaning uniform. A spotlight blasts on, blinding her. Her head pounds, and someone is calling her name, over and over.

"Willa! Willa, please! Can you hear me? Willa!"

When Willa opens her eyes she's in a hospital room.

CH. 27

BEWILDERED AND ALONE, WILLA GATHERS details like a spider monitoring its web. Her head hurts. She fell. She was on the boat and now she's not. Her arm hurts, too, because there's an IV pushed into her elbow; the medical tape keeping it in place itches. There's a blanket over her body and under her arms; it's blue and thin and scratchy. The ceiling is gray; the walls and floor are white. A curtain is pulled closed to her right, cutting the room in half. It has a hideous floral pattern. A machine beeps behind it. She's not alone then, yet she is. Where is Lane? Her family? A doctor or nurse? How long has she been here? How did she get here? What happened? *Where is Lane?*

She takes a deep breath to push back against the wave of panic. She gathers more details. There's a small, square window. It's sunny outside. There is a counter next to the bed; on the counter is a vase filled with purple flowers. Her phone is... Where is her phone?

When Willa tries to sit up, she finds that she can, though it makes her head throb and the room spin. There's a remote sitting on her bed, white and attached to a cable; it has a red button. She pushes the button, just to see what will happen.

What happens is, a nurse comes in. She's wearing scrubs printed with colorful cartoon cats; her hair is in long braids dyed bright red, and she wears lipstick that matches. She asks Willa a bunch of weird questions, shines a light in her eyes, takes her blood pressure, and tests her reflexes. Then she calls in a doctor, who does all of the same things.

"What's your name?" The doctor asks again. She has short gray hair and half-glasses perched on her nose and thin, serious lips.

"Willa." Don't they know that already? She scowls with frustration. "Where's Lane? What happened to us?"

But everyone who comes in her room wearing scrubs or a white coat has a million dumb questions and no answers. When they finally leave, Willa scoots to the edge of her bed and swings her legs off the side. She waits for the blinding pain and wave of nausea to subside. She needs to find her clothes and then get someone to take this itchy, irritating IV out. Then she can check out and go find Lane. Only, when she goes to stand, her stomach lurches, and stars swim across her vision.

"Whoa, hey." It's Lane. Lane's on crutches with her ankle wrapped in a peach-colored bandage, but otherwise she's okay. "I don't think you should be getting out of bed," Lane says—*Lane is here*—hobbling over to Willa's bed and gently pushing her shoulder back.

"You're okay," Willa says, going wherever Lane wants her to, back into the stack of thin pillows and under the scratchy blue blanket.

"I'm okay," Lane confirms. "Are you okay?"

Willa shakes her head, it makes tears well up in her eyes from the pain. "I don't know; they won't tell me. They won't tell me anything." She sounds whiny and small, like Amelia when she wouldn't take a nap until Mom found her stuffed bunny.

Lane sits gingerly on the edge of the bed. "Okay," she says in a soothing voice. "You're okay." Willa nods miserably, and Lane pushes sticky-damp strands of hair from Willa's forehead. "You fell after you ran up to fix the sails, remember?" She waits for Willa to search her addled mind and continues when Willa nods carefully. "Well, they said you got a concussion and you blacked out. I got you down to the cabin and radioed for help, but by then the storm had mostly passed,

120

so I was able to use the remaining lower sails that you got up and make it back to land."

She remembers. The storm, the boat, her phone dropping into the ocean, Lane jumping on board. "The mast broke. The mainsail fell. I fixed— I did it?" She fixed something?

Lane's smile is fond and wide. "You fixed it. You saved us."

Willa smiles, though it sort of hurts to do that, too, and Lane grins back. Though Willa missed the storm passing and the sun coming out, Lane's face is close enough.

"Anyway," Lane says, clearing her throat. "The coastguard met us as we came on shore and transported you here. Which is Nags Head by the way. We drifted up pretty far."

Willa lets this all sink in. "And you?" She glances down at Lane's dangling feet.

"Just a sprained ankle from jumping onto the boat. And a little humiliation since I was in my underwear when they found us. That was horrible." She blushes and looks at her knees.

"I mean, someone seeing you in your underwear is definitely worse than getting a concussion," Willa snarks.

Lane's eyes narrow; her tone is playful. "I'm glad you can see that. Absolutely worse." Her smiles slips though, and she fixes her gaze on the wall. "I was so worried about you."

Willa takes Lane's hand; her skin is smooth and warm under Willa's cold, dry fingers. "I'm okay," she repeats. "I'm sorry for... Well, all of this."

Lane squeezes Willa's hand. Her thumb comes up to stroke Willa's knuckles. She finally looks away from the wall, nervously settling first on Willa's eyes then Willa's mouth and then their joined hands. "The thing is I—"

"Willa!" The door clanks open, the sound like a stake through Willa's head, and her mom rushes in, immediately coming around the other side of her bed and engulfing Willa in a hug. "Oh, thank god, thank god, oh, my god." She pulls away, squashes Willa's cheeks in her hands and puts her cry-smiling face centimeters away from Willa's. "If you ever," she says, in the same joyfully relieved voice, "Pull a stunt like that again, I swear to god I will—"

"Well, I should go," Lane pipes up. She snags her crutches from their resting place against the counter. "I, um. I'm glad you're..." She nods.

"Wait," Willa says, but her mom interrupts, "Thank you again, Lane. I'm so grateful that someone level-headed was there to save her. What would she have done without you? Oh, I can't even think of it!"

It's stupid and irrational, but Willa goes tense with irritation at her mom's gushing over superhero Lane saving the day. Maybe Lane finds something intriguing about Willa's stupidly impulsive nature, but she's the only one. Lane sends Willa a look that seems to be an apology, or pity more likely, then she swings out on her crutches. What was Lane trying to say, *the thing is I*— What? She what? And on the boat, before the mast snapped, weren't they about to—

"There are some people here to see you," Christina says, standing to fuss with the blanket and plump the pillows. "They've been very worried about you too." She's trying to smile, to look as if she's perfectly fine, happy even, but Willa's seen that look on her face, the one she had when Willa would catch her at the table, crying, with bills spread across the surface. It was how she'd look after working two overnight shifts, then still somehow muster the energy to take Willa to the beach or the park. Or, when Willa was older, how she would look when Willa told her not to come to school for career day.

"Mama," Willa says, a term she hasn't used in a decade. "I'm sorry."

Her mom flutters her hands in dismissal, then starts crying in earnest. Her mom's life has changed so much—new husband, new kids, new city—that Willa forgot it wasn't so long ago when they were each other's whole entire world.

Christina pulls Willa to her again; her lilac perfume and soft chest are home for Willa more than any cottage or island will ever be. "I love you," her mom says, voice thick and tears wet on Willa's hair. "All of you, just as you are. I hope you know that, sweet pea. I always will, no matter what." Willa nods against her chest and releases a long, trembling breath.

Then the door bangs open again.

CH. 28

"WILLA, YOU ABSOLUTE LEGEND!"

Bodhi bursts into the room; she's tan and sun-bleached blonde and the smattering of freckles on her face has expanded into constellations. Bathing suit straps peek from her tank top and above the waistband of her low-slung shorts. Bodhi in the summertime is Bodhi in her best, sand-speckled form. "Everyone is taking about how you sailed off into a storm and almost died trying to save the boat and how you and Lane, uh—" She glances at Willa's mom, who is still sitting at the end of Willa's hospital bed. "Well anyway, everyone is talking about it."

"Great," Willa says. "Super."

Bodhi frowns at Willa's flat tone. There was a time when Willa would have been thrilled to be "an absolute legend" and even more stoked that everyone was getting the details wrong, believing that she went off in a storm on purpose, that she didn't just slip and hit her head but nearly died while saving the day, and that she and Lane, found in her underwear, did more than just kiss briefly. And it's not just because everyone found out the truth about her sailing abilities in the most humiliating way, but because, on that boat with Lane, before the mast broke and everything went sideways, she had a glimpse of being liked and wanted just for herself. She wanted that. No bullshit, no lies, no perfectly filtered alternate reality. Just her.

"Bodhi," Willa says, pushing herself up off the pillows until it hurts too much. "I need to tell you what really happened. Like, all of it."

Christina stands, wipes her eyes, and smooths out her sundress. "Well, I'll go let Tim and the kids know you're okay and check on your discharge status, Willa." She nods to Bodhi, and the look they exchange makes Willa wonder what they've said to each other, what they may have talked about while sitting in a hospital waiting for Willa to wake up.

"First of all," Willa says, twisting the scratchy blanket covering her lap. "I am sorry for lying to you. It honestly started when—"

"Wills." Bodhi chops a hand through the air. "It's cool; it doesn't matter."

"It *does* though." It matters that she comes clean and starts fresh. Maybe it's just the bump on the head talking, but she can't understand how she did it for so long or why it mattered to her, juggling all of the lies, desperately needing to be some idealized version of herself. It was exhausting. "I let you think that I was someone I'm not. And if you don't want to be friends anymore, I understand." Willa stares down at the folds of blanket clenched in her hands while Bodhi stands silently. It would break her heart to lose Bodhi; there's nothing fake about how much she means to Willa.

After what feels like forever, the mattress dips next to her. "Willa," Bodhi says, with so much kindness that Willa can't look up. "I was upset at first, okay, and yeah, you told us some stuff that wasn't true and that put you in danger, which was stupid." Willa nods miserably. It *was* stupid and dangerous. She starts to apologize again, but Bodhi cuts her off. "But I'm over it. It's all good, dude."

It shouldn't be good though. "You're only saying that because that's just how you are. I'm a fraud, Bodhi. I've been lying to you and your moms for years. I lied to get a job. I lied about hurting my shoulder. You don't even know me, not really."

Bodhi coils one long, tanned leg beneath her and tucks her hair behind her ears. It reminds Willa of so many late-night talks: the two of them piled into Willa's bed curled up together, talking about everything and nothing for hours on end. Why didn't she say something then? Why did she let everything go on for so long?

"Wills, listen. Maybe you're right that I need the truth about some stuff, but I do know you. I know your *heart*." Willa shakes her head, but Bodhi continues. "I know that if there's only enough coffee for one cup left in the pantry, you'll save it for me. I know that you'll always cover a shift for me at the shop, no questions asked. I know that whenever you pick up food from somewhere, you'll always get something that I like so we can share it. I know that you can't hold your liquor, and when you're drunk that you like to cuddle." Willa smiles a little, and Bodhi knocks their knees together. "I know that you always remember my birthday and my moms' birthdays *and* their anniversary. I know that you are always up for anything, no matter what hare-brained idea I come up with, because you are seriously the bravest, most balls-out person I have ever known. Who else would enter a *fucking intense* professional regatta after learning how to sail like, a couple months before? No one but you, Willa."

Willa grins. "That was pretty wild of me, wasn't it?"

"Hell yeah, it was."

It seems that while she was busy trying to be someone else, Bodhi saw her anyway. Bodhi was her best friend no matter what.

"Bo, you're, like," Willa voice cracks. *God, how many times can I cry today?* "Like my sister, even though I have a sister, but she's a baby and only says like five things." She sniffles. "You know what I mean."

"I do, yeah." Bodhi curls up next to her with her head resting on Willa's shoulder. She smells like sunscreen and bug repellant and sunshine. "So... You and Lane..."

Willa brings Bodhi's arm over her stomach. The truth is, she likes to cuddle all the time though she only lets herself do it when she's drunk. "Nothing happened. We got rained on, and some waves were coming overboard so that's why we didn't have clothes on." Bodhi makes a disappointed noise. "I mean, we did kiss." Bodhi makes an interested noise. "But that's it."

"Boo." Bodhi gives a thumbs-down.

"I really like her though," Willa admits. "Really, really like her."

Bodhi taps Willa's hip. "Then what's the problem?"

The last several months of trying to figure out what Lane really thinks about her seem just confusing now. If she hadn't been so insecure, she could have just asked. "I thought she was into you," Willa says. "And *she* thought *I* was into you."

"Yeah?" Bodhi's voice is way too smug for Willa's liking. "Everyone wants a piece, and I can't say that I blame them."

Willa laughs; it hurts her head but it feels great. "Shut up."

"You know I'm all about free love," Bodhi says, smug in a joking way now. "The more the merrier. I'm into it. I say we do this."

Willa groans. "Ugh, why am I friends with you?"

"Best friends," Bodhi says, squeezing her tight.

Willa smiles against her soft, sunshiny hair. "Best friends."

CH. *29*

WILLA'S NEW DOCTOR AT THE hospital is a soft-spoken old man with sparse white hair and the fine bones and stature of a very large, very thin bird. He reminds Willa of Mr. Rogers, if Mr. Rogers had become a doctor who was still practicing well into his eighties. He has a cardigan buttoned up beneath his white coat and everything.

"How about we try to walk in a straight line, just as far as you feel comfortable," Doctor Pascal says, in a voice so gentle and kind and soft that it makes Willa burst into tears.

"I'm sorry," Willa says, crying harder because she's crying and doesn't know why. "This ke— keep—" She sniffs. "—keeps happening."

"Oh, it's quite all right." Dr. Pascal stands, patiently stooped, next to her bed. "Concussions can cause mood swings; it is to be expected."

After she stops blubbering, Willa scoots to the side of her bed and stands, holding on to the railing as the room spins. Her mom bought her some warm socks from the gift shop; Willa wiggles her toes against the fuzzy insides.

"Are you feeling dizzy?" Dr. Pascal asks, his just-above-a-whisper voice nearly drowned out by the whooshing of blood in Willa's ears.

"Yes. And my head hurts." An understatement. Now that she's on milder painkillers, her head feels as if someone is intent on driving the entirety of her brain out through one ear with a pickaxe.

"Well, that is also to be expected. Whenever you're ready, dear. No rush."

Dr. Pascal makes her walk in a line, back and forth. Then she has to spin in a slow circle with her arms stretched out. She touches her nose with one finger while her eyes are closed, then stands on one foot, then the other, then she has to hold her hands out flat as though she's carrying a pizza and count to ten. When Dr. Pascal pushes against her raised arms and tells Willa to push back, she's more than a little afraid that she'll break the man right in two. He's stronger than he looks.

"Now," Dr. Pascal says, after testing her muscle tone and coordination, then her reflexes, vision, and hearing. "Do you remember what happened?"

"Yes." Willa settles back in bed, dizzy and exhausted. "We were on the boat in a storm. There was a loud noise, and I ran up to check on it. The mast broke, and I fixed it, but then I fell because it was wet and slippery, and we'd been drinking wine."

"And after that?" Dr. Pascal's hands are splotched with gray-brown spots, Willa stares at them as she tries to think.

"After that... I was in the hospital."

Dr. Pascal *hmms* and writes something on Willa's chart. "You regained consciousness in the ambulance."

"I did?"

"Mmhmm. Says you were asking about someone named Lane. That you were worried about her because she'd hurt her ankle. You didn't seem aware of your own injury." Dr. Pascal looks up from his notes. "Does that sound familiar?"

With some effort, Willa shakes her aching head. Could Bodhi be right? Is she a better person than she's been giving herself credit for? Or was it just the concussion talking, that she was focusing on Lane because she was confused and afraid?

"Some memory loss is normal," Dr. Pascal continues. "Yours is very minimal, I wouldn't worry. In fact, I do believe we can release you to go home."

At that, of course, Willa begins to cry.

The cottage has been emptied of spring-break tourists early, most likely thanks to Christina's insistence. It probably cost her grandparents a good chunk of money, which Willa will certainly hear about once she's better and which makes her feel guilty, as if she got a concussion on purpose. Her mom stays in the cottage for several days, sleeping on the pullout couch in the living room and bustling about the kitchen making meals that Willa doesn't eat. Mostly, Willa sleeps: all day, with the curtains drawn tight and a blanket crammed against the bottom of the door to keep the light out; all night, only waking to use the bathroom and take the pills that make her even sleepier. Her head hurts, always, endlessly.

"You call me if you need anything at all," Christina says to a groggy Willa. Her life and family back in Kansas City can wait no longer; Tim has to go back to work, and Christina has no one to watch the kids all day. "Or I can stay. I'll figure something out—"

"S'fine," Willa slurs it into her pillow. "I'mma sleep anyway."

A kiss lands on the top of Willa's head, and she sleeps.

"Okay, sleeping beauty, medicine time." Bodhi shakes her awake. It seems as though a second has passed since her mom left, but that was in the morning when it was bright and it's dark now. A sliver of moon is revealed in the tiny crack between the drawn curtains. Willa sits up, holds her hand out for the pills then for a glass of water, clutches Bodhi's arm and shuffles to the bathroom, and feels a tiny bit better. Her head hurts a little less. She's a little steadier on her feet, a little less confused about the day's events.

"Was Lane here?" Willa walks back to her room under her own power, just with Bodhi's hand at her elbow as a precaution. She vaguely recalls hearing Lane's voice earlier.

"Yeah. She brought you a plant and a coloring book." Bodhi waits until Willa gets situated in bed, then flops across the end of it.

A plant and a coloring book. "Oh. Okay."

Bodhi shifts to her side and props her head up on one bent arm. She grins. "Yeah, a plant because she was worried the stronger smell of flowers might aggravate your traumatic brain injury. And a coloring book because you can't do jack squat and she thought you might get bored. That is, once you're done being a total zombie."

"Oh. Well. That's... thoughtful." Willa pats flat the blanket lumps next to her. "Can I have them?"

Bodhi bounces up off the bed. "Sure."

The plant is a squat succulent with purple-tinted leaves in a terra-cotta pot; the coloring book is titled *Zen Coloring* and is ocean-themed.

"Dude," Bodhi says, flopped onto the end of Willa's bed once again. "She's way into you, right?"

Willa shrugs. It's too confusing for her to parse right now, when sorting out how to flush the toilet is challenge enough for her. She's hurting and sluggish and under a heavy fog of prescription painkillers. But when she thinks of Lane, she can't help the smile that stretches across her face and the warmth that settles in her chest.

"I'm tired," she tells Bodhi. After she leaves, though, Willa is able to stay awake for a bit. She touches the pointed ends of the plant and smiles.

CH. 30

AFTER ONE FULL WEEK OF being totally headache-free, Willa does a deep clean of the cottage, catches up on bills since Bodhi hasn't paid a bill on time in her entire life, and replaces some worn-out light bulbs in the bathroom. Willa crouches precariously on the counter, one knee on the raised lip of the sink and the other wedged between a giant bottle of aloe and a decorative candle—sea-breeze scented, of course—as she screws in the new bulbs and notices that the toilet has been running lately.

Willa and this toilet go way back; she can remember being small enough to crouch between the tub and the toilet bowl holding a flashlight while her mom replaced a valve or fixed a leak, snaked out a clog or reattached the flapper. She already has a hunch as to what's going on before she lifts the lid to the tank: The fill valve is broken. Willa fiddles with it, hoping she's wrong and it's an easier fix, but no luck. She turns the water supply off and goes to the tiny hardware store. She walks, not quite ready for her skateboard.

"Hey, Willa, you get that ceiling fan fixed up all right?"

The hardware store is little more than a large storage space with rows of white metal shelves stacked to the rafters, with sawdust and potting soil scattered on the concrete floor. There's a key cutting station next to the analogue-style cash register, and behind it rises a wall of cubbyholes containing various washers and knobs and specialized screws. It smells like plant fertilizer and varnish, and Ms. Purcell has been running it for longer than Willa has been alive, taking over for her parents who ran it for their whole lives.

"Yes, ma'am," Willa says, her accent slipping stronger to match Ms. Purcell's coastal Southern drawl. "I'm here for a fill valve today." The capacitor she needed for the fan had to be special-ordered and took forever; she hopes the valve is standard and she can get it today. The water bill is going to be bad enough as it is.

She's in luck. Ms. Purcell rings her up after they find the valve Willa needs, painstakingly punching in the numbers on the little orange sticker. "I was real sorry to hear about all the troubles you've had lately," Ms. Purcell says, moving her finger over the price tag and then back to hover on the keypad. *1...*

Willa's neck goes hot with shame. She doesn't know if Ms. Purcell means the whole race debacle or the boat stealing or sailing off into a storm or nearly cracking her skull open, but she doesn't ask. Probably all of it. "Uh, thanks." *8...*

"Well, take it from an old lady: Some day you won't even care about all that mess." *9...*

"No?" Willa bounces on her toes.

"No, no." *5.* "That'll be nineteen... ninety... five." Willa doesn't correct her, fishes out a twenty and tells her to keep the change; god knows how long it would take her to get a nickel from the drawer. Ms. Purcell slowly bags the part and then slowly rips off the receipt and slowly hands over the bag. Willa is nearly hopping in place. "If you aren't making mistakes, are you really living?" Ms. Purcell says.

Willa smiles. "No, ma'am."

She swings the bag at her side as she walks home, happy to be free from pain and out of bed, though the sunlight still hurts her eyes even through sunglasses. She doesn't know what's next, where she goes from here, but for now Willa is happy to be here at all. Maybe, she thinks, as she rounds the corner to her quiet street, she's gained a little perspective, a little more confidence, a second chance. Maybe even a girlfriend.

She's got the tank open, the water drained out, and her hair twisted into a lopsided bun when the doorbell rings.

"Oh. You're up." Lane looks surprised, then relieved, then awkward, moving back on the porch and crossing her arms low on her waist. 'Well, I just came to check on you, so…"

It's as if they're playing the world's dumbest game of romance chicken where the loser confesses their feelings first. "Well, here I am," Willa says.

Lane rubs her arms and looks up at the sky. "Right."

"Do you want to come in?" Willa asks, and Lane says, talking over her, "What are you doing right now?"

"Fixing a toilet."

"Sure, yeah."

"Okay," they both say, at the same time again.

Willa leads her to the bathroom where the toilet sits empty and exposed. Music streams from Willa's brand-new phone, which, between financing a new one and still being on the hook for the old phone that she dropped into the ocean, she will likely be paying for well into old age. Lane perches on the edge of the bathtub. She's dressed casually, in shorts and tank top; her shoulders are pink and dusted with freckles, as if she's been out in the sun a lot lately. Willa envies her. That dark room was making her feel like a trapped animal.

Willa grabs her wrench and has to scoot past Lane to loosen a bolt on the underside of the tank.

"Shouldn't you call a professional for this?" Lane says, eyes wary. "What if you break something?"

Willa locks the wrench in place and tugs. "If I break something then I'll fix that too. You aren't really living if you aren't making mistakes," she tells Lane, just as the bolt comes loose.

Lane raises her eyebrows but says nothing else as Willa works. Technically, she doesn't know what she's doing, but she did watch a few YouTube videos and there are also instructions on the package. It's easy enough, until she can't seem to get the fill cup positioned right;

the little tab she's supposed to easily click into place is in a fiddly spot that she can't quite maneuver.

"Wouldn't have taken you for a Veruca Salt fan."

"Huh?" Willa is literally elbows-deep in the toilet, hunched over the tank with her messy bun coming unraveled. "Volcano Girls" blares from her phone. "Oh, the music? Yeah, my mom was big fan of theirs. I guess I grew up listening to classic stuff like that."

"Oof," Lane says.

It takes Willa, preoccupied with the latch that won't latch, a minute to realize what she said. "I mean, like, they had a pretty long career." Lane is not her mom's age, though she is closer to it than Willa had considered. Not that it matters, not to her anyway. "I like a lot of types of music. Old stuff, new stuff." Willa says as she struggles with the fill cup. "Though all I seem to listen to is jam bands when Bodhi is around, and they all kinda sound the same to me? Though I guess they're really a live band, which sort of defeats the pur— *Ugh, why won't this thing latch!*"

Lane, who had been watching Willa struggle with what looked like bemusement-meets-concern, stands up. "Need some help?"

Willa wants to say no, but she does need another hand to keep the fill cup in place while holding the lever out of the way so she can push the latch into place. "Yes, please."

Together they get the new fill valve installed, and Willa turns the water back on to test it. She flushes a few times while Lane watches, her mouth tipped up into a pleased smile. "You know I was never really allowed to do that."

"Fix toilets?"

Lane laughs a bit. "No. Make mistakes. If I wasn't perfect, then why bother, right? And look what it's gotten me. I just gave up. I'm trying to unlearn years of this shit, and you just—" Lane laughs again, but it's humorless. Willa doesn't know what to say, afraid to break the spell of Lane being open, that maybe this is it, this is the moment when they finally clarify what they are to each other. "But you— You fall and you get up and you fall and get up, over and over and over and ov—"

"I don't fall *that* much," Willa protests.

"I just mean." Lane's mouth presses flat. "I mean, I'm trying here, okay. Undoing this stuff at my age is hard." Her eyes on Willa's are beseeching, and Willa doesn't know *exactly* what she wants Willa to do, but she does get that Lane needs time, and Willa can give that to her. It's a step somewhere, at least, even if it isn't moving them forward.

"Yeah. Yes, that's okay."

Lane's shoulders relax. "Are you hungry?"

 CH. *31*

THINGS MOSTLY RETURN TO NORMAL. Willa has a tough conversation with Jenn and Robin, though it's easier than she expected. They "sort of knew" she couldn't really sail. After all, they'd watched her sail that one evening and, though they were proud of her hard work, they said, she didn't look like someone who had been sailing her whole life minus some time off for an injury. In the end, they said they were disappointed but still wanted her to continue working at the shop. And they still care about her, of course, and are glad she's okay. For Willa, it seemed like the best she could hope for.

Willa wakes once again to the mournful song of the ferry beginning its early morning route. She sits up, swings her leg over. She gets up slowly; sometimes she gets dizzy if she stands up too fast. *Does it ever get tedious*, she wonders for the first time, how the ferry leaves port on the same schedule day after day, week after week, year after year. Does the captain ever wish they could just mix it up once in a while? Go late or early or even not at all? Willa pads across the gritty hardwood floor, past Bodhi's bedroom and the predicable sleeping lump of Bodhi in her bed.

She gets ready for the day, hops on her board, and coasts out of her street with the sun on her face, the wind at her back, and a shiny new helmet strapped tight beneath her chin. She passes the small, older cottages of her neighborhood. She glides past the upscale condos, the pastel vacation homes, the clutch of buildings housing the general store and hardware store and gas station, the municipal building, and the small elementary school. She passes the same restaurants and hotels and shops and cafes.

Though she often thinks of the island as unchanged, frozen in time, the beachfront businesses shift every few years. New facades replace old ones when ownership changes hands. Some are gutted and redone completely, like the Cordova's real estate business that was once a yogurt shop. Porter Sails, in fact, was a kite store when Willa was kid. They sold fancy kites made of bright fabrics with long tails that spiraled in the wind. *What happened to the owner of the kite shop*? she wonders. She'd never thought about them, as if once off the island they ceased to exist. Jenn and Robin might know, but then it doesn't really matter; the fancy kite store and the sail shop aren't so different. What an odd hobby, catching the wind. Willa takes a wide left turn and glides on.

The shop is the same, busy now that summer is in full swing. Every once in a while, a customer will squint and tilt their heads and ask her, "Hey, are you…" Yes, she'll tell them, she's that girl who entered that race. Yes, she really did get disqualified before it began. No, she hasn't gotten back on a boat yet. Otherwise, she keeps her head down and does her job. In the evenings she and Bodhi party with the same people they've always partied with. Hunter has become a more regular fixture. Willa has yet to brave Instagram. Everything is more or less the same, except for Lane.

They have a standing lunch date, usually at The Sand Dollar but sometimes at the little sandwich shop that has a few picnic tables scattered outside in the sand and sometimes at The Oyster Bar, which is where Willa heads today. She gets a table on the patio that's painted pastel green and blue and yellow, where Caribbean music jangles from the outdoor speakers. Summer is in full swing on Porter Island, packed with people and buzzing with bright energy. Willa orders a sweet tea; she presses it to her neck and cheeks before taking a drink.

"Hey." Lane appears, kisses Willa on the cheek and slides into the tall chair across. She's been off her crutches for a while now; her sprained ankle is completely back to normal. "Sorry I'm late. Showing went long." She rolls her eyes.

"Regular obnoxious clients or extra special obnoxious clients?" At lunch, Willa usually gets all the salacious details of Lane's annoyingly rich and just plain annoying clients who are shopping for beach houses. Lane orders a white wine. Super obnoxious then. "They complained about the roof pitch being too high. The house is amazing and that's not even a thing. A too-high roof pitch. They were just being insufferable because they can." Over the course of their lunches, Willa has learned that Lane really, really hates her job and is not great about hiding that fact from anyone, including her clients. "Which I told them," she says, with a slight cringe. "So they switched to my brother."

"Well that's—" Willa starts, but stops herself from saying their loss, because Lane's brother is apparently very good at being a realtor, and Lane is, well. Good at other things. "On to the next one," she says encouragingly. Lane drains half of her wine.

The waiter takes their orders and collects their menus. "Speaking of my family," Lane says, face pinching as if her last sip of wine turned sour on her tongue. "My parents are in town."

"Oh?" Willa was starting to wonder if they really existed.

"Yeah. I was actually, um…" Lane wipes the condensation off her wine glass and nibbles her lip. "I was wondering if you wanted to meet them?"

Taken aback, Willa doesn't immediately answer. She and Lane have been circling around each other for weeks. Willa has been giving Lane space to figure out what she wants, which is fine. Totally one hundred percent fine.

Except at these daily lunches Lane will catch her eyes and smile, as if she's pleasantly surprised to see Willa there, every time. And Lane will kiss her on cheek when she arrives and peck her on the lips when she leaves, blushing and rushed. She always texts Willa in the morning first thing and then at night, just to chat. And sometimes when they walk from the restaurant to the car, Lane will catch Willa's pinkie with her own and, if no one is around, kiss her hard up against the side of Lane's car, leaving Willa wound up and bewildered. Sometimes Willa can't shake the feeling that she's a practice girlfriend, as if Lane is merely training extensively for the real thing.

"You don't have to meet them. I just thought— Anyway, forget it. No biggie."

Willa took too long to answer, and Lane is clamming up. Her arms are tucked into her lap and her gaze is fixed on an empty table. Surely asking Willa to meet her parents means something. "I do want to. I sort thought they weren't real people is all."

Lane laughs. "Yeah well, they sort of aren't." Willa raises her eyebrows in question. "You'll see. So was the shop busy today?"

After lunch, Willa goes back to work, thankfully for only a couple more hours. She's distracted and clumsy, bumping into customers on the floor and zoning out at the register. She goes to the back to grab a pair of high-performance racing boots in size nine and ends up staring at the rows of boxes stacked tightly on the shelf for an indeterminate amount of time.

"Willa? Are you okay, honey?" Jenn pokes her head into the stockroom. "If you need to go home, we can manage."

Since her concussion, she's had a ready excuse to blow off just about anything: work, cleaning the cottage, making people leave the cottage when she's had enough of them but Bodhi hasn't. It's as simple as saying her head hurts, and everyone will rush to let her off the hook. She feels fine though. And more than that, she doesn't want to be the sort of person who makes excuses anymore.

"Oh yeah, I'm okay." She grabs the shoes she came in for and hustles back to the store. If she's been waiting for Lane to be ready, to make the first move toward something real, surely this it?

CH. *32*

LANE SENDS A TEXT TELLING Willa to dress fancy, which is something Willa definitely does not do. She has a pair of jeans that aren't a total worn out disaster and a white, button-up shirt printed with tiny cheeseburgers that Willa only bought at a yard sale because she thought it was funny. She lays out the okay-ish jeans and the cheeseburger shirt and frowns. She's pretty sure it doesn't qualify as fancy. She asks Bodhi for help, and she pulls out a variety of sundresses made of thin, gauzy fabric. Willa tries them all on; each one brings a new wave of despair and self-loathing. On Bodhi they look effortlessly sexy: breezy and summery and clinging just right. When Willa looks at herself in the mirror, she's reminded of how they learned about the Great Depression in school, how people used to fashion flour sacks into dresses.

It's Hunter who comes through for her, dashing off to her condo and returning with fitted slacks in shining emerald green and a loose, button-up shirt that does not have cheeseburgers printed on it.

"We could do something with your hair?" Hunter gathers the mass of curls into both hands. She stands behind Willa, and Bodhi stands behind her.

"My hair does what it wants," Willa says, tucking and untucking and re-tucking the shirt.

"Tucked," Bodhi says.

"How about…" Hunter tucks Willa's hair into a low twist, then asks Bodhi to grab bobby pins from her purse. She secures everything as if she's done this a million times to Willa's hair, then pulls a few tendrils loose to curl in spirals around Willa's face. "Yes."

"Hot," Bodhi proclaims. "Lane's gonna love it."

Willa's heart rate ticks up. She hopes so.

She's meeting Lane at the ferry, which they'll take to Oak Island for dinner at a yacht club. Willa has always viewed the yacht clubs that dot the shores here with suspicion. Exclusionary and exclusive, with their private beaches and private docks, they're the sort of places people probably join in order to look down at other people—people like Willa. Her stomach is in knots, gets worse when Lane's white SUV drives in, then loosens entirely when Lane steps from the car. Willa doesn't dare draw breath as Lane walks toward her in a little black dress and sharp heels, with the wind blowing her hair back, hips swaying, chin held high. Willa is certain she's had a fantasy exactly like this.

"Hi," Lane says.

Willa garbles something in response. She waits for a kiss on the cheek that doesn't come.

"Ready?"

Willa nods and notices, now that she's through being gobsmacked by Lane, the look of sheer panic in Lane's eyes. She slips her hand into Lane's and gives it a squeeze.

Lane blows out a breath. "Okay."

Willa's hackles are up already, more so when Lane drops her hand as the ferry approaches the shore, even more when Lane walks ahead of her down the sidewalk and up to the yacht club. Inside, everything is muted and quiet and starched white; glasses and silverware tinkle gently; conversation is at a low murmur. A host in a tuxedo asks for their reservation.

"Cordova," Lane says, and looks at Willa as if she wants to apologize to her. "We're meeting our party here, actually."

Their party is a dark-haired couple that Willa recognizes from the picture on the boat. They're older, with lined faces and softer bodies, but unmistakably Lane's parents.

"Mom, Dad, this is Willa. Willa…"

They stand to shake Willa's hand, then sit and delicately place their starched white napkins back over their laps.

"Nice to meet you. Sorry I broke your boat," Willa says, immediately getting off on the wrong foot by bringing up the boat incident. "My bad."

"I hear you had quite the adventure," Lane's dad says. Chip. Who knew there were really people called Chip? "Please, sit."

They order a calamari starter and fancy wine and exchange niceties. Willa watches Lane to see what fork to use and how often to sip her very dry wine.

"Are you old enough to drink wine?" Lane's mom asks, expression pinched.

"Oh, yep," Willa says, and Lane mutters, "barely."

They order entrees with price tags that make Willa feel a little faint. It's pleasant, stiff, in the way that chatting with someone you don't know and have very little in common with is, but pleasant. Willa can't work out why Lane was so nervous, and even now next to Willa is stiff and closed off and barely speaks at all.

Then Lane's mom—*call me Marie*—says, "So you two are dating? Is that what this is?"

Lane's eyes widen, and her face drains of color. Marie waits for an answer with a cold look and raised eyebrows.

"Now, Marie…" Chip says, but doesn't finish the thought.

Willa, worried about Lane, and still used to lying as a reflex, laughs. "Oh, gosh, no. No, we're just friends, right, Lane?"

Lane glances at Willa, at her parents, then pats the corners of her mouth with her starched white napkin. "Excuse me," she says and strides purposefully toward the bathroom. Willa turns to call after her, and just barely manages to catch the way Lane's face shifts, from stoic to crestfallen, just before she pushes the bathroom door open.

Willa says a word that's probably banned at this yacht club, and chases after her. "Lane? Lane, are you— God, this is a nice bathroom." The sinks are all gleaming chrome and marble, and the lights are dimmed; there's even a sitting room with leather couches. Willa bends to look for shoes beneath the spacious cherry wood stalls. She spots Lane's black heels in the very last one; every other stall is empty. "Hey, it's me," Willa says, knocking softly. "Willa," she adds, as if Lane may have been expecting someone else to join her in the bathroom. The lock clicks, and Lane lets her in. Lane stands back against the door, making Willa shuffle to one side in order to stay clear of the toilet.

"Everything okay?"

"Yeah, I—" Lane shakes her head. "That was dramatic, sorry."

Getting Lane to be vulnerable sometimes feels to Willa as though she's fishing with a single strand of silk; anything other than gentle patience and Willa loses her. "I just wasn't sure what to say," Willa starts. "I didn't mean to upset you."

"It wasn't you." The stall is cramped enough that Lane's hand brushes Willa's hip when she gestures, and the smell of her perfume, powdery and floral, fills Willa's nose. "Actually, I brought you here because…" Willa's breath catches; here it is, she's finally ready. "I was hoping to borrow some of your courage."

Willa blinks, pushing back against disappointment. "Oh."

"It's just I haven't come out to them, and it'll be a whole thing and—" She drops her head back against the door and groans. "I'm pushing forty and I can't tell my parents that I like girls. It's pathetic."

"Hey." Instinctively, Willa moves closer, putting a comforting hand on Lane's arm the way she would for Bodhi, only Bodhi's skin isn't so soft and so warm and so electric under her palm. "You aren't pathetic. Don't get me wrong, coming out is important, and you'll feel a million times better not carrying around this secret, but also, if your parents are gonna be shitty about it then don't. You don't owe your true self to shitty, unsupportive people."

Lane's tense shoulders relax. She smiles a little. "When did you get so sensible?"

"Must have been the bump on the head." Willa should probably move away, drop Lane's arm, and give her some space, but she doesn't. "And you're plenty brave. You jumped off a dock onto a moving boat. And you kept a cool head, then sailed us out of a storm."

"That was different. We did that together."

"Still…" Is the stall getting smaller? Is that why she's close enough to Lane to feel the heat of her body? "I think you're plenty brave."

Lane licks at her bottom lip and says, "yeah," in a tone so low and husky, Willa feels it in her belly. She leans, heat pulsing through her, close, closer—Lane's lips brush hers—and stops.

CH. *33*

"Lane, I— I don't know what you want from me." Doesn't she need some sort of clarification? Shouldn't she and Lane establish some idea of what this relationship is or isn't?

Looking at Willa's mouth, Lane says, "I don't either." She closes her eyes and swallows. "Not friends. Not that."

Lane lifts a shaking finger to Willa's lip and traces the shape of them, and Willa's protest dies before it ever began. She is only human. "Not friends" is good enough for now. Willa lunges forward, taking advantage of the solid door behind Lane to push up against her. There is nothing curious or exploratory about this kiss, nothing cautious in the way her hands grip Lane's hips, no over-thinking at all in the way Lane's fingers twist in Willa's hair.

Willa thinks of suggesting they take this elsewhere, like somewhere that isn't a bathroom in a snobby yacht club, but the process of cooling off enough to face Lane's parents, finish dinner, and take the ferry all the way home is not realistic. Pulling away from Lane's hot, pliant mouth and soft, sweet sighs is an impossibility. Lane nudges her tongue past Willa's lips, arches her back, and moans loud enough to echo in the gleaming marbled space. Willa is just starting to wonder how exactly how far this is going to go when Lane answers that question by working open the buttons on Willa's shirt.

The bathroom door scrapes open; footsteps clack across the floor outside.

"You look really good tonight," Lane whispers, mouth pressed to Willa's ear. "Really, really good." She moves back, presses a finger to her own lips, then kisses a line down Willa's neck. Willa squeaks. Cool air hits her chest and stomach as Lane gets her shirt open. She drags her lips across the exposed curves of Willa's breasts. A toilet flushes. Willa takes advantage of the background noise and whines with need. Lane's hot mouth is so close to her peaked, stiffened nipples but just skimming them, teasing.

Whoever is in the bathroom with them takes their sweet time fussing at the sink. They wash their hands and dry them, then open and close containers—probably makeup—spray pungent, chemical-heavy perfume, and put on lotion that smells like oranges. All the while Lane is driving her crazy with her mouth on Willa's mouth, then her neck, her ears, her chest, until Willa is strung-tight with desire, and is this close to yelling at the person to get the fuck out already—*how much fucking lotion does one person need?*

Lane's hands begin to grow bolder, releasing Willa's hair to push her shirt down off her shoulders, trailing down to trace her breasts and skim across her stomach before beginning to fumble with the button and zipper on Willa's dress slacks. Finally, their bathroom companion leaves, and Willa is out of patience. She yanks Lane forward and spins them around, backing Lane into the oversized, fancy toilet paper holder, which gives her leverage as Lane sits partly on top of it. The angle is perfect for Willa to hike one of Lane's legs around her waist.

She doesn't want Lane to give in to self-doubt, to disappear inside of her own head and get lost in her insecurities, so Willa unceremoniously shoves the bottom of Lane's little black dress up over her hips, runs her hand up the back of Lane's hitched leg and around to the inside of her thigh, then up to trace the seam of her satiny black underwear.

"Good?" Willa whispers, to check in. Lane swallows hard and nods, then wiggles the top of her dress down to her waist. There's no bra beneath for Willa to fumble off, so she kisses Lane instead, caressing her breasts with one hand and with the other pushing aside the thin strip of satin to where Lane is slick and swollen.

If anyone else has entered the bathroom, Willa doesn't know and doesn't care. All she can hear is the way Lane is panting and whimpering. She can only see the way Lane's back curves and her hips shift and her mouth falls open. All Willa can feel is the slick heat of her clenched around her fingers. And when Willa goes to her knees on the hard bathroom tile, the salt-bitter-sweet against her tongue is the only thing she ever wants to taste.

Lane comes, shuddering against Willa's mouth and making a racket as she chants *oh, oh god, oh* and clambers along the walls for something to hold on to. Willa coaxes her through the aftershocks until Lane goes limp and slides off the edge of the holder. Willa stands, rubs at her knees and smiles at her handiwork: Lane slumped against the wall, dress reduced to bunched fabric around her waist, eyes closed, and mouth turned up in bliss.

"*God*," she says. "That was—" Her eyes are bright and wild, like a kid on Christmas morning. Willa can guess what she's feeling; she remembers the first time she felt the same way, realizing that sex could be *like that*.

"Can I?" Lane says, tugging her clothes back in place. "To you?"

"If you're su—" Is all Willa gets out before Lane is pinning her against the wall.

*   *   *

WILLA TRIES HER BEST TO sit with Lane's parents and act as if nothing at all transpired in the bathroom.

"I was feeling sick," Lane tells them, as if that might explain why her cheeks are red and her lipstick is long gone, why her dress is wrinkled and she's absolutely parched, slugging down a glass of water while her mom looks on with a peeved expression.

Willa's hair is in a state. The updo that Hunter so expertly crafted is now completely undone. Willa hasn't a clue how to fix it, and after Lane tried to help by making an attempt at a ponytail that looked more like a frizzy feather duster, Willa decided it was best to leave it loose to do what it may, which is be a disaster, mostly.

"Well, I'm glad you're feeling better," Chip says.

Lane replies, "Oh, I am," in a way that makes Willa choke on her mineral water.

They finish dinner, decline dessert, and wait for the check in relative silence. Next to her, Lane is significantly more relaxed, and Willa is still in shock that they did that. Here. Just now.

"This is such a nice club, isn't it?" Marie says. Despite the pleasantness of what she said, she's looking at Lane as if she angry. "It's not too late, Laney."

Lane's body language shifts back to stiff and uncomfortable. "I don't want to join the club. I already told you." With some effort, she cracks a smile.

Marie's answering smile is chilling. "You know," she says the same fake-pleasant way, "I would think that after all we've done for you: Welcoming you home with open arms in spite of the way your sailing career ended, giving you a job at the family firm even after you swore for years that you would never demean yourself by working there—"

"I never said—"

Marie goes on as if Lane didn't speak. "And all I ask in return is that you humble yourself *just a little* to return the family name to good standing amongst our friends and associates. There is a regatta coming up, and the club could use someone with a little clout. Minus that whole ugly incident at your last race, mind you. I'm *sure* most people have more or less forgotten about that. But still, you could redeem yourself! Don't you want to erase that *awful* experience?" She looks down, pressing a hand to her heart. "Don't we just want the best for you?"

"I don't think you do," Lane snaps. "Let's just be honest with each other. For once." Lane's chin lifts in challenge, and the tension is as palpable as the stench of that woman's horrible perfume that still clings to Willa's clothes.

Willa doesn't know where to look; she holds her breath as she waits for someone to speak and glances at Lane and then Marie and at Chip, who is scowling and muttering at the check, seemingly oblivious. Or, perhaps more likely, he's purposefully oblivious. Lane takes a breath, as if to stand up for herself, finally say what she's been trying to say, then lets the breath out and hunches in her seat. Under the table, Willa slips her hand into Lane's and holds tight.

"Did sales tax go up?" Chip says. "I think they're trying to hit us with some extra fees."

"I'm gay," Lane blurts. "I like girls, women, I—" Chip and Marie stare at her. Willa holds her hand tighter. "I don't care what anyone here thinks of me. I don't care what you think of me. All my life I have been afraid to be myself because you convinced me that the only thing that matters is what other people think of me, but screw that. I'm gay and Willa's gay and we don't give a fuck!"

The people at the table next to them gape, wide-eyed, then turn away, moving food around their plates but not eating, trying to appear as if they aren't listening to—and judging—every word Lane says.

"I'm bi actually," Willa cuts in. "Or pan maybe? Bodhi likes 'fluid' but personally I need something a little more solid in terms of identity? It's really like, a gray area, for me anyway—" Lane's parents stare at her blankly. "And that's probably a conversation for another time. Lane? Are we running late for the ferry? Don't want to miss the last one." She widens her eyes at Lane, desperate to leave as soon as possible.

Lane gets it. "Yes, right." She stands. "Also, I sold my boat. And, I don't want your job, or your support, or— or your yacht club dinners, not if any of it comes with conditions. Not if it means I'm still afraid to live my life how I want." Willa stands, too, and tugs at her hand. They start to walk away, but Lane pauses and turns, adding in a softer voice. "I'm sorry if this hurts you, but I hope that someday you can understand."

CH. *34*

WILLA FEELS THE WEIGHT OF dozens of eyes as they leave the restaurant. Lane's head is held high, and her shoulders are squared as she forges confidently ahead, and Willa wonders how close she is to breaking, how tightly she must be holding herself together before she can safely fall apart. Will she let Willa be there? Or will she close off, shut down, and pull away again.

Her own coming out had been unceremonious; after some off the cuff remark from her mom about Willa having a boyfriend someday, Willa had added, "or a girlfriend." And her mom blinked, corrected course, and said, "or a girlfriend, yes." Willa was twelve, and that was that.

It's not until they're at the ferry port, waiting at the empty dock next to idling cars with their interior lights turned on, that Willa asks, "Are you okay?"

Lane turns, presses her hands to her mouth, and *beams.* "That. Was. Amazing."

Across the sound, a ferry lumbers toward them. "Yeah?"

"Yes." Lane stretches her arms out wide and throws her head back to smile up at the star-speckled sky. "Like a huge weight has been lifted; you have no idea."

She does though. Not that particular weight, but hasn't she been dragged down by the heaviness of her own secrets? She's been tethered to the bottom of the sea and drowning from the weight of her insecurities, her fears.

"Now what?" Willa asks. The ferry is a few feet from the dock; the final journey is always done in increments. It has always seemed so impossible to Willa, how something that huge can slot into place so gently: this giant thing churning in the water only to nudge itself right into place at the lip of the dock.

"Come over?" Lane says. She's the most ebullient Willa has ever seen her. Free.

There are boxes stacked against a wall in Lane's living room and just a few stacked up, orderly and neat, near the TV. Willa wants to ask, but she doesn't get a chance because Lane switches on a dim lamp and stands in front of Willa with her back turned. "Unzip me?"

The zipper is one of those unobtrusive types meant to blend in with the dress; it's small and inefficient in Willa's fingers, slipping and getting stuck as she drags it down Lane's back. Her knuckles brush the smooth, muscled skin of Lane's back, and, when the zipper makes it down to the sinuous curve at the base of her spine, Willa lingers, stroking across a spot that she's thought about so many times. "You're gorgeous," she whispers, no longer bothering to keep that thought to herself.

Lane catches the dress against her chest just before it falls. "Thank you. I've never really—" She shakes her head, stopping herself from dismissing the compliment. "Thank you."

Willa understands now, after meeting her parents, why Lane of all people would feel as if she isn't enough or worthy or beautiful. And here they are, the two of them, finally standing on solid ground after spending so long near-drowning in self-doubt, and Willa can feel it, as Lane turns and presses a soft kiss to Willa's lips, that something huge and scary is slotting itself delicately in place just right, as if it was always meant to land just there.

I'm falling in love with you. She doesn't say it. Not yet.

Lane is gentle this time, the earlier thrill and desperation giving way to slow drags of her lips between Willa's with her hands cupped almost reverently around Willa's face. Lane breathes out slow sighs; her body bends into Willa's like the tide coming in. Lane's dress falls, and she steps out of her shoes, then asks, "can we?" and looks toward the hallway leading to her bedroom.

Lane undresses Willa and takes her to bed, shyer than she was back at the yacht club, yet not as awkward as she was the first time they tried this, when she was so sure she'd be terrible at it and was convinced that Willa didn't care about her at all. It's much too soon for Willa to tell her that nothing could be further from the truth, but Willa tries to show her.

They wind together, side by side and naked, kissing with so much want that Willa's jaw soon begins to ache and her skin buzzes with heat. Lane moves back, and Willa curls over her, sliding her legs between Lane's spread thighs. Willa ducks to curl her tongue around Lane's nipple; Lane whines and begins to rock her hips, and Willa moves back up to kiss her while her hips grind down against her. Lane's kisses grow erratic and distracted; just her lips rest against Willa's mouth as she gasps and ruts. She begins to tremble, back arching, vocalizations loud and uninhibited.

Willa comes, shuddering, body humming and content until she realizes that Lane is shaking and shaking and not quite getting there. Willa nudges her onto her back, pushes her knees wide, and presses deep inside her with three fingers, working them in and out, then four, fucking Lane with them. Lane's skin shimmers with sweat, and her back is strung as tight as a bow, just on the cusp of release. Willa presses in, twisting her hand and searching with her fingertips until she feels the raised spot that makes Lane's hips twist up off the bed, then she curls her fingers back toward herself and rubs her thumb against Lane's clit. Lane comes and comes, grabs Willa's wrist when she starts to pull her hand away, and comes again.

"Jesus," she says, several minutes later, with her arms curled up behind her head, body loose, and smile wide. "I think I could go for a cigarette and I haven't touched one in almost twenty years."

Willa laughs, but feels a little strange about the statement. She doesn't often notice the age difference between them, it doesn't matter to her at all, but Lane lived a lot of her life before Willa came along. Does that make her a blip on Lane's radar? An affair she'll soon look back on fondly? Willa pushes the thought away.

"I'll take that as a compliment," she says lightly.

Lane's grin stretches wider. "You should."

Willa isn't sure what level of cuddling is appropriate, but she snuggles close enough to rest her cheek on Lane's shoulder. "Did you really sell your boat?"

"Mmhmm," Lane says, eyes drifting closed. "I feel like… A new person."

Willa frowns. Maybe she doesn't want Lane to be a new person. Maybe she likes the person that Lane already is. "So what happens now?"

"We'll see." Lane tucks her face into Willa's neck, presses her lips in a lazy, open kiss there. "We'll see."

CH. *35*

WILLA IS RIPPED FROM A deep sleep by a sudden blast of light. She groans and yanks the covers over her head, hoping to escape the painfully bright light. She has a flashback of recovering from her concussion, when sunlight felt as if it was cracking her skull into pieces. She peeks out to chance a look, letting the brightness in by increments, checking the clock on Lane's nightstand. She groans again.

"Rise and shine!" Lane chirps, pulling back the covers and waving a cup of coffee in front of Willa's nose. "We should do something today; are you working?"

Willa cracks one eye open. "Yeah."

"Well, call in. I feel like being irresponsible." Lane bounces onto the bed with way too much excited energy for this early in the morning. Or ever. "Oh! I know, let's go clubbing! I've never done that."

Willa opens her other eye and pushes up off the pillow. "It's seven in the morning."

"Oh. True." Lane sips the coffee that she brought for Willa, and given the way she's nearly vibrating it's likely not the first cup she's had this morning. "Hmm, okay." She bounces again, thinking. A few drops of coffee dribble down the side of the mug. "Oh! I know, do you have drugs?"

Willa sits up. "*What?*"

Lane slurps more coffee. Willa takes it from her. "No, never mind," Lane says. "I have a better idea. Get dressed, come on!" She throws last night's clothes onto the bed. Willa sighs and texts Bodhi to see if she can go in early today and cover her shift.

Lane's "better idea" turns out to be having Willa teach her how to skateboard, only she rejects Willa's offer of a helmet and her advice to stay near the grass, then insists on starting on the top of a hill by herself.

"This is not a great idea," Willa says, shielding her eyes from the sun as Lane stands with one foot on the board. There's a strange flip of their dynamic now, Willa the sensible and serious one, and Lane recklessly forging ahead without regard to consequence.

"How do I jump with it? Like off those stairs?" Lane calls.

"You don't."

Lane waves off the response and puts her other foot on the board.

"Told you," Willa says later, cleaning Lane's knees and elbows with antiseptic pads while she sits perched on the closed toilet in her bathroom. "No jumping."

"Oh, you're no fun," she hisses as Willa swipes at the scrape on her hand. "Okay, so what's next?"

"What if we… stay in and watch a movie?" Willa smiles hopefully. If Lane keeps going at this rate, she'll end up with a concussion to match Willa's.

"*Ugh*, no."

Willa frowns. She isn't sure what's gotten into Lane, whether she's freaking out about what went down last night and is keeping herself busy to avoid thinking about it or is overcompensating to make herself think that everything is fine or—

"Come on, Willa. For the first time in my life I feel like I can do anything I want. I've missed so much. Please?" Lane's eyes are wide and beseeching, and she pulls Willa into a deep kiss that leaves them both breathless. It's not as though Willa can say no after that.

"Let me stop by home and change first."

*   *   *

"Well, well, well look who finally made it home." Bodhi spins around on a bar stool like an evil mastermind welcoming their minion. "And where have you been, young lady?"

"Hilarious." Willa slams the door shut behind her. "A real laugh riot."

"Wait." Bodhi's teasing smile slips away. "Did you not have fun?"

"Yes, I— I dunno." She slides onto the stool next to Bodhi and steals a piece of toast from her breakfast; god, she is *ravenous*. "I guess I was hoping we could talk about stuff, like figure out where I stand, what our relationship is, but we mostly just had sex."

Bodhi lifts an eyebrow. "And this is problem because..."

Willa sighs and steals a bite of scrambled eggs. Bodhi must have gone grocery shopping. "I'm not like you, Bo. I'm not good at the casual thing. And Lane has spent her whole life being all *serious* and *committed* and *responsible* so now she's going all out in the opposite direction."

Bodhi nods sagely. "Mid-life crisis."

"She's thirty-six, Bo."

"Exactly."

Willa rolls her eyes. "Anyway, she wants to 'do something crazy,' whatever that means," Willa does air quotes and hops off the stool. "So I'm gonna change and stuff." Hopefully it's not something that involves more bleeding, or clubbing, or *drugs*, for Pete's sake.

"I might have an idea."

Willa pauses at the door to her room. "If you say threesome I swear to—"

"No." Bodhi tips her head. "Well— No. Something else. Bring your helmet."

Summer weather hits Porter Island hard. That's great for beach goers, not so great for standing on the highest dock on the island where the sun beams hot all around them, on the dark-painted boards beneath their feet, reflecting on the water below, heating their stooped backs and exposed skin as they set the skateboard at the beginning of the dock.

"Now," Bodhi announces. "The low railing will stop the board, but there's enough space between it and the top railing for you to fit between and be launched into the water." She nods to Lane. Lane sits on the skateboard and claps.

"And what if it doesn't?" Willa says, apparently the only person here with any sense, which is terrifying because she does not have very much of it. "What if *she* hits the railing instead? What if there isn't enough room? What if the board goes flying into the water too? What if only the board goes into the water?" Bodhi shrugs. Willa tries to appeal to Lane's usually more reserved nature. "Lane, before you do this you should know that Bodhi is by far my least-smart friend." Bodhi protests with a *hey!* and shoves Willa's shoulder. "Okay, but seriously, this is not a good idea."

Lane grips the edge of the board and leans forward. "That's the point."

"Okay, but what if—"

"Willa." She sits back to squint up at her. "I got one *B* in school, ever. I used to go from studying to training to studying to competing. I didn't do stuff like this. I wasn't really living. I was just existing. I think I need to get this out of my system, one way or another."

Mid-life crisis, Bodhi mouths. Willa gives her a look.

Despite Willa's worry that Lane might *not* live through this, she relents. "Fine, but you're wearing the helmet." Willa secures it on Lane's head, as if it will make a difference when she goes hurtling twenty feet through the air and into the ocean.

"Now it's usually night, and we're usually drunk..." Bodhi says, a statement that should probably go without saying. "But since it's only nine o'clock in the morning, a blindfold will have to do. It's more fun if you can't see the water coming."

Fun for whom, Willa wants to ask. She settles for crossing her arms disapprovingly.

"All right Wills, we're gonna push on three. One…Two…"

 CH. *36*

No one dies skateboarding off the pier. It doesn't work as well as Bodhi promised, since most attempts involved them literally shoving Lane through the railing and into the water below. Lane seems satisfied, though, and Willa has to admit seeing her run back up the beach and down the pier, soaking wet and laughing, is well worth the risk. Hunter joins them after a while, and she, Bodhi, and Lane climb over the railing, stand on the edge holding hands and free fall into the water together. Willa leaves them to it and takes her board to a hotdog stand a little way from the pier.

"Four, please." The guy working the stand is the son of the woman who owns it. Willa remembers seeing him as a kid when she was an older kid; he'd hang out nearby while his mom worked. Willa leans against the building as she waits for the food; her face is turned up to the sun. Sometimes she wonders if it's sad that she's spent nearly her whole life on this little island off the coast of North Carolina, but on days like this, when the sky is cloudless and clear, and the ocean settles on her skin and lips and fills her lungs, why would she ever want to be anywhere else?

Arms full of footlong hotdogs, Willa turns to go in the direction of Lane's raucous laughter, then spots Lane's parents coming out of an art boutique several doors down that sells seashell wind chimes and blown-glass fish sculptures. As she's trying to decide what to do—Hide?

Wave? Skate off as quickly as she can in the opposite direction?—Mr. and Mrs. Cordova come her way.

"Yo!" The kid at the hot dog stand calls. "You forgot your change."

Dammit. Willa shifts the hotdogs into the crook of one arm and against her chest to collect her change, which the kid counts out slowly into her hand, "Seven sixty… seven sixty-five… seven sixty-six…and seven sixty-seven. Have a blessed day!"

Willa spits out a thank you and hops back onto her board and— "Oh. Mr. and Mrs. Cordova. Hello." She all but skates right into them.

Chip is on his phone; he gives Willa a nod. Marie lifts her chin and squints. "Oh, yes. Hello. Ella, was it?"

"Willa."

Marie's lips purse. "Mmm." She's dressed as if she just came from an art gallery in the big city instead of a kitschy, beach-themed souvenir shop; she's wearing layered designer clothes that are inappropriate for the weather and oversized sunglasses.

Willa wants to say something like, "You have no idea how amazing and brave and beautiful your daughter is, and it's your loss." Or, "Why would you make your child spend her whole life chasing your love and approval? What will it take? Shouldn't you just love her? Isn't that what a parent does?" Or maybe just, "You suck; I hope you know that." Instead Willa stutters and finally comes up with, "Uh. Nice here, huh?"

"Maybe so," Marie says. "If it weren't for the heat and humidity and the mosquitoes and the hurricanes. I don't know anyone can *stand* to be here year round."

And it isn't anything Willa hasn't complained about herself—hell, she probably would have added tourists and sandflies and lack of a decent grocery store—but Porter Island is her home. She's *allowed* to complain about it. Marie Cordova, who buys and sells vacation property here, who owns a huge, gorgeous home right by the water that she barely lives in, whose most persistent personality trait is her absence, does *not* get to. Anger bubbles in Willa's chest, and she knows, rationally, that she isn't entirely angry about Marie's complaints. Luckily for Willa, thanks to her grandparents, she speaks fluent passive-aggressive.

"Well, good thing you'll be gone soon. You usually are, aren't you?."

She pushes off and immediately gets stuck on a raised section of sidewalk. The skateboard comes a sudden stop, and Willa stumbles off, clutching the hotdogs as she tries to stay on her feet. Ketchup oozes out from the foil wrapping on one of the hotdogs and smears onto her shirt.

"Now, hold on a minute, young lady."

Willa turns, and all the fight goes out of her. Reflected in Marie's giant rose-gold tinted sunglasses, Willa sees herself as the Cordovas must see her: some kid on a skateboard in board shorts and a dirty T-shirt, with wild hair and nothing better to do on a weekday afternoon but goof off at the beach. Just like that, all of her insecurities come rushing back. What can she offer Lane? What sort of life can she build with someone else when she's only just beginning to discover what sort of life she wants for herself?

"I have to go, sorry."

After eating and lying on the beach for a while to dry, Willa convinces Lane to go home and take a nap. Judging by the dark circles under her eyes, she probably didn't sleep much—or at all—last night.

Lane changes into a tank top and underwear and nothing else; she's sweet-smelling and warm in bed next to Willa. "Can we fool around when we wake up?"

"Sure," Willa says, though she doubts she'll sleep. Lane snuggles close, and, without meaning to, Willa stiffens. She moves away.

"Are you okay?"

For the first time in a long time, Willa lies. "Yeah, I'm fine."

Bodhi texts later with an invite to a bonfire at the beach near her place, which means drinking, which means Lane is extra excited. "Will there be... *marijuana?*" she asks, whispering the illicit word.

The fire is burning steadily when they arrive. The usual group plus some summertime extras are gathered around. "So, you do this all the time?"

"Yeah," Willa says, but doesn't tell Lane that it's getting old, that sometimes she wonders what the point is and who else is just going through the motions. It used to be one of the many ways she validated herself, *see all these people want me around*, only now it feels hollow. If she never came to one of these beach parties again, they'd continue without her all the same. Willa nurses a beer and watches Lane.

"Your girlfriend is having fun, huh?"

Willa slides Hunter a look. "Not my girlfriend."

"Oh. Well, whatever."

Willa is automatically irritated whenever Hunter is around and she can longer remember exactly why. The spoiled rich girl thing, sure, but lots of their friends are rich and don't bug Willa in the same way. Maybe it's because she just seems to always be around, inserting herself wherever Bodhi is. Maybe Willa was insecure and wanted to Bodhi all to herself. Willa looks at Hunter, clocks the way she looks at Bodhi, the way they look at *each other* lately, and she gets it.

"Ugh, I'm gonna miss this," Hunter says, randomly.

"Why? Giving up cheap beer and bong hits for Lent or something?"

Hunter starts to reply, then stops. The fire flickers orange across her features. Lane is now drinking beer from a funnel. "She didn't tell you."

"Who didn't tell me what?"

Bodhi comes stumbling up the beach before Hunter can answer. "You guys, we should tie the skateboard to Colin's truck and take it to the boat launch— What?" Hunter communicates something with her eyes and a flick of her head. "Oh. Yeah, I guess I got sidetracked today."

Down the beach, Lane whoops and dances and then trips, falls down into the sand, and laughs hysterically. Willa needs to take her home soon.

"Someone want to fill me in?"

"It's just—" Bodhi looks nervous, worried even. It's so strange. *Bodhi*, nervous. "I got into this program I'd been thinking about applying to. Hunter really encouraged me, cuz I, I dunno, just assumed I wasn't good enough, I guess. Anyway, I'm gonna go to school for forestry and wildlife conservation. Be a park ranger and shit."

"Wow." Willa isn't sure why Bodhi was so afraid to tell her. She's surprised of course, she didn't know Bodhi had been considering going back to school, but being a park ranger, tromping around outside and sharing the joy of nature with other people, makes total sense for Bodhi. Then it dawns on Willa. There's no college on Porter Island. "Online?"

Bodhi and Hunter exchange a look. "Well, that's the thing—"

"You're leaving." Of course she's leaving. Bodhi's roots here aren't as deep as Willa's, and she'd mused before about leaving, though never seriously. Never for long. Willa just thought… Well, she'd hoped Bodhi didn't mean it. Now she has to find a new roommate. She'll have to work with some stranger at the sail shop. She'll lose her best friend. Willa starts to tear up and she can't blame a concussion this time. For the past five years it's been her and Bodhi, thick as thieves, two peas in a pod, and now—

"Aw, Willa, don't cry. I'll just be a ferry ride away, and then a short little drive, right down in Wilmington." Bodhi tugs her into a hug. "Nothing will change, not really."

It isn't true, and they both know it. "Yeah," Willa says. "Sure."

"Willa! Will! A!" Lane yells for her again, not far enough away to warrant her current volume. "Let's go skinny dipping!" She starts to tug off her shirt.

"I better—"

Bodhi releases her. "Yep. Go."

As she tucks an arm around Lane's waist and talks her out of skinny dipping, Willa wonders idly if this is the last ever party she and Bodhi will attend together. It's the inevitable and bittersweet end to something that Willa was ready to let go, yet it still hits, sharply, in the center of her chest.

She manages to get Lane home, and thank god it isn't far because Lane is doing very little to help them get there. Willa fishes Lane's keys out her pocket, and Lane giggles.

"Buy me dinner first, will ya?" She pauses, then splutters with laughter. "Oh, my god, will ya. Willa. *Will ya*. Get it?"

"Yes, I get it." Willa steers her into the condo and kicks the door closed. "Why don't you go lay down, and I'll get you some water and something for the headache you'll have in the morning, okay?"

Lane chirps, "Okay!" then collapses onto her couch.

Willa meant the bed, but close enough. She pours a glass of water and searches Lane's cabinets until she finds a bottle of ibuprofen and returns to find Lane snoring and draped awkwardly half-on and half-off the couch. Willa sighs and sets the water and pills down. She carefully moves Lane's dangling leg and arm up onto the couch, and covers her with the throw blanket that always sits neatly folded on one end. Her heart aches when she thinks of all the times she's done this for Bodhi, aches more at Lane's serene face and the soft murmurs as Willa tucks her in. Even though she's being kind of stupid right now, Willa is completely crazy about her.

"Willa." Lane's eyes fly open.

"Yeah, I'm here." She'll stay. She doesn't want Lane to wake in a panic, not remembering what she did or how she got home.

"Willa, Willa, hey." Lane reaches for her, putting her palm on Willa's cheek after some clumsy fumbling. "If you were ten years older..." Lane says and pouts. It's cute.

Willa answers as if Lane was telling a knock-knock joke. Maybe she is, she's pretty drunk. "If I was ten years older... who?"

Lane doesn't joke back or laugh, just looks seriously into Willa's eyes so intently and for so long that Willa starts to squirm. Lane closes her eyes. Willa straightens up from the couch. A joke with no punchline, then. Knock-knock. Who's there? Nobody. Then Lane mumbles, so slurred and quiet that Willa barely catches it.

"Then I could tell you the truth."

CH. *37*

WILLA PLANS TO WAKE UP early and bring Lane some greasy food to help with her hangover, but when she shuffles from Lane's bedroom into the living room to grab her shoes and go, she finds Lane already awake dressed in workout leggings and a long tank top and eating a bowl of cereal on the couch.

"Oh. Morning." Willa stops in her tracks near the front door. "Feeling okay?"

Lane wobbles her head from side to side and swallows. "I'm alive. I think."

"Well, that's something." Willa smiles, then steps into her Vans. Now she has time to go home before work and maybe catch Bodhi for a bit, since their days are officially numbered now.

"Hey, if I—" Lane looks down at her cereal and swirls the spoon around a few times. "If I did anything last night that was, uh—"

"It's fine," Willa cuts her off with a flick of her hand. "You were drunk. I'm not going to hold anything you did against you." *Or said,* Willa thinks. Whatever Lane meant by "the truth," Willa should probably let Lane keep to herself. After all, if she wanted Willa to know, she'd tell her when she was sober.

"Okay. Thank you," Lane says, relief evident in the lift of her mouth and drop of her shoulders. "I think I may have overcorrected a little there." Lane sets her bowl down on the coffee table and tucks her legs up and to the side. She looks so sweet, so softly lovely in the morning light, that Willa has to fight an overwhelming urge to kiss her and take her back to bed.

"Maybe a little, yeah."

Lane hums. "Well, I'm gonna go do some yoga. Try to re-center myself." She drops her legs to the floor and stretches. "I'll, uh. I'll call you?"

"Sure."

Willa stands there a few beats too long. It's just because of Bodhi's imminent departure weighing on her mind, probably, but the moment seems heavier than it should. Maybe it's the reality that things have shifted between her and Lane, and, in the sober light of a new day, neither of them knows what comes next. Or if they do, neither one is willing to say it.

Bodhi isn't at the cottage when Willa gets home, but there is a message on the answering machine that must be from her grandparents, because no one else uses the landline and leaves messages on the answering machine.

"Our first booking is the second week of June," her grandmother's recorded voice says as Willa waits for a bagel to toast. "And I'd like for you to give all the rooms a fresh coat of paint. God knows what those walls have seen. Oh, and let me know if the exterior needs to be power-washed. I couldn't remember how long it's been, though I do believe I have asked you to take care of it many times, and also if you can trim…"

"Hi, Grandma, so nice of you to call! How am I? Oh, things have been a little tough lately but you know me, I just hang in there no matter what! Thanks *so much* for your concern!" Willa butters her bagel and pours a glass of juice. The message drones on, and Willa continues her imaginary one-sided conversation with her grandmother, who didn't even bother to start her message with a *hello*. It's either that or start to worry about where she can crash and that for the first time ever she'll be dealing with all of this—getting the cottage ready for vacationers, finding a place to stay for the summer— alone. She hopes the shop is busy today so she doesn't have to think about anything at all.

Unfortunately, she walks into a quiet store and is surprised to see both Jenn and Robin in the back, sitting at the break table with a guy who looks to be in his mid-thirties, with a ruddy complexion and blond hair swooped to one side. Willa eyes them suspiciously as she clocks in.

"Who's the Chad-looking dude?" Willa asks Robin when she joins Willa in the front of the store, referring to guy's overall yacht-club, former-fraternity-president vibe.

"That's Mr. Kelley's nephew, Max."

"Oh, yeah, now I recognize him." He used to come help Mr. Kelley in the summer, scraping barnacles and fixing up old boats. It's been years since she's seen him. "Wasn't he working in finance for a big corporation in Charlotte?"

"That's right." Robin moves away to refold a display of T-shirts, and Willa can't help but feel as if she's being cagey about something.

"So... What's he doing here?"

Robin pauses with a T-shirt held up to her chest. She seems to choose her next words very carefully. "With Bodhi leaving soon for school, we realized we needed a little more help around here. Jenn and I— Well, at some point in the future we'd like to take a less active role in the store and so—" She finishes folding the shirt, sets it down and pats it, as if to be completely sure it isn't going to randomly unfold itself. "Max moved here recently and is looking for something a little more low-key than what he was doing before, and we need a manager, so."

That guy is going to be her boss? Someone who's never worked at the sail shop a single day, who breezed into town after deciding he was bored raking in barrels of money in the big city? Who probably drinks vintage scotch with people like Chip Cordova, chortling at the riffraff that can't afford to set foot in their private beachfront yacht clubs? *That guy?*

She is losing everything. Just not at all in the way she thought she would. Panic claws at her chest; her mind scrambles for a way out. They can't just turn the shop over to this guy and leave her, not Robin and Jenn too. *They can't.* "What about me?"

Robin frowns. "Willa, you'll be fine. In fact, we're counting on you to show Max the ropes. You probably know this store better than I do."

"No, I mean—" Willa steps around the counter, tries to hold herself the way Lane usually does: confident, competent, mature: shoulders squared and chin lifted. She even lowers her voice a bit. "What about me for the manager position?"

*   *   *

LUNCH TODAY?

She texts Lane during her first fifteen-minute break while sitting outside on the short dividing wall between the shop and the marina. Robin and Jenn agreed to let her apply for the manager position, and she's so excited that she has to tell someone. It feels good. It feels right, as if she's finally making a mature, adult decision and choosing her path forward. Just like Bodhi.

I'm at a hot yoga class on Oak Island. Sweating out this hangover. Rain check?

Willa worries a little at Lane's text back—is she really at a class and can't make it or is she blowing Willa off now that's she's come to her senses? She shakes off the thought and starts to dial her mom's number instead.

"Willa! Hey!"

Willa glances up, shading her eyes to see across to the marina, where Mr. Kelley is waving at her. He motions her over, so Willa pockets her phone and jumps down from the wall.

"Got your boat back, finally. You'd think the poor ol' girl was involved in a multi-national money laundering scam instead of a little bump-up." He claps Willa on the back and points out the boat she'd tried—and abysmally failed—to race.

"It's not my boat, Mr. Kelley," she reminds him.

169

"Well, it might as well be! Any time you want to use 'er again just go right ahead." How a man as nice and generous as Mr. Kelley wound up with such a terrible nephew, Willa does not know. Of course, she doesn't know Max like, at all, really. Still, she's certain he's terrible.

"I appreciate it but I think my sailing days are done."

Mr. Kelley rubs his leathery red face, considering Willa. A seagull skitters around their feet on the dock, no doubt scavenging for scraps of food or fish. Willa has half a mind to punt the thing right into the water.

"I think your problem is that you were only sailing to prove something. You gotta try setting sail for the joy of it." He spreads his arms out in front of him, palms up, as if setting them onto the line between the sea and the sky, holding up the horizon. "Joy is a good enough reason do to something, you hear?"

Mr. Kelley hasn't always owned this marina. For most of Willa's life it belonged to the same older couple; it was a family business that they had every intention of passing on to their kids who were a few years ahead of Willa in school. But their kids left, like a lot of the people Willa grew up with. Off to bigger and better things, or so they always thought. Whenever anyone came back to island after a stint away, Willa always took it as a warning that there really isn't anything better out there and that she was smart to stay, that she was right to keep her life so small. Really, she was afraid. That's where it all came from: the lying, the fake persona, wanting desperately to be someone she wasn't. It was fear, not bravery as Lane thinks, that always propelled her forward. But what if…

What if, instead, she actually *was*.

What if she was brave?

For the first time, Willa looks out at the ocean and the horizon that she's been looking out at for nearly all of her life and wonders what else is out there for her. For the first time she allows herself to feel the tug of longing for something different and the possibility that she can actually have it.

"Yeah," she tells Mr. Kelley. "Maybe so."

CH. 38

BODHI AND HUNTER ARE IN Wilmington looking for an apartment, so Willa is on her own getting the cottage spruced up. She puts on her rattiest T-shirt and shorts and tugs a ball cap over her curls, then goes down to the utility closet beneath the raised deck out back. She squeezes around a weed whacker and old window screens and avoids getting snared by a hose coiled on the ground. On a shelf behind bottles of weed killer and ant killer are partially used cans of paint; the colors inside are revealed by the drips caked almost artfully down the sides. After some thought, Willa chooses three: soft blue, pale yellow, vibrant green. She tucks pruning shears under her arm and gets to work.

She doesn't mind the labor required to get the house in shape: painting and cleaning and repairing any wear and tear inside, mowing the lawn, snipping the deadened ends of the pink-flowered azalea bushes, and cutting back the unkempt wax myrtle bushes outside. She likes making the place shine, highlighting its best attributes and hiding its flaws. In fact, she's really good at it. In the backyard, she picks up sticks and gum pods and re-hangs the hammock that they'd put away when the temperature started to drop. She enjoys being productive, doing something that engages her body and mind and gets her outside in the sun. Maybe that was part of the appeal of sailing. Maybe that was what Mr. Kelley meant. She's halfway through painting the living room in a shade that matches the sky when her phone rings, interrupting her painting playlist. She wipes her hands on her shorts and scoops her phone from the counter.

"Hey, Mom."

"Hi, kiddo. You sound out of breath, everything okay?"

"Oh, yeah." She pushes a sweaty clump of hair back under her hat. "Just painting before summer vacation season starts."

Her mom tsks. "Why they don't just pay someone to do that…"

"I don't mind," Willa says. She rotates her shoulders in turn to work out the ache from so much repetitive movement. It makes her feel as if she's earning her keep. It makes her feel connected to her mom, too, who always rolled up her sleeves and did what needed to be done.

"So where's the dynamic duo?" Willa asks. It's quiet in the background way out in Kansas City, an unheard-of occurrence. Christina has been calling or texting often since her visit, and usually their phone calls are punctuated by Atticus and Amelia wanting to say hi, wanting to video chat so they can show off or use the goofy phone filters, or else whining and fussing.

"Oh, I had Tim take them to the park. It's finally getting nice here. I miss the island most when it goes from freezing rain to regular rain to tornadoes here."

Willa's stomach twists with guilt. Her mom is sitting inside, calling her, instead of enjoying a rare nice day with her family. "You should be out there with them, then."

"Willa," her mom says, in a warning tone. "It's okay to need me too." It's something she's been repeating a lot lately, that Willa is trying to take heed of.

"I know. Okay. So…" Willa grabs a soda from the fridge and catches her mom up on the events of the last few days: how Bodhi is leaving soon, that Robin and Jenn are looking for a manager and she has decided to apply, about Lane's parents being the worst.

"And how are you and Lane?"

Willa picks at the tab of her soda. "We're not… Not really anything."

"Hmm," her mom says. There's the sound of door sliding open then closed, as if Christina has gone outside to enjoy the weather after all. "You know, she came by when you were out of it."

Willa smiles to herself. "I know. She brought me a coloring book and a plant." The little succulent is still in her room, on the windowsill where it can greet the sun every morning.

"Not only then. Every day. She'd sit by your bed and just quietly stay with you, for hours sometimes."

Willa warms at the thought, even as she dismisses it. "She was just worried."

"Well, some people aren't great at saying how they feel," her mom responds. "But they show you. So if you're unsure of where you stand with Lane, next time pay attention to her actions, not her words. I think it'll be pretty obvious then."

They chat about how things are going on her mom's end: the funny things the kids have said, how Tim's job is going, the recent commissions her mom has gotten for the jewelry boutique she started just before Atticus was born that's finally starting to take off. And though she's not sure if it's true, her mom's words about Lane's actions revealing her true feelings linger throughout the rest of the phone call and while Willa finishes painting. It's similar to something Bodhi said, back in the hospital when Willa was concussed: that she knew Willa's heart, despite the lies she'd told. Does Willa really know Lane's heart? Has she tried to?

Lane texts her that evening, when Willa is soaking in an Epsom-salt bath trying to ease the burn of her overworked muscles. *Dinner, my place?*

The sun is low and lazy in the sky when Willa arrives at Lane's with her skateboard tucked under one arm and most of the paint splatters scrubbed away. Willa scrapes at a blob of green paint on her thumbnail while she waits for Lane to answer the door.

Out back, she texts. Willa looks around, as if trying to see around the row of high-rise condos, and walks backward off the porch. "Out back" is the beach and the ocean. *What is Lane up to?* Willa winds her way down the wooden path that cuts through long sea grass and down to the beach, where Lane is sitting on a blanket with a picnic basket set on one corner. Her mom's words ring like a bell as Lane smiles and stands.

"I think I owe you a nice dinner after ambushing you with my parents."

"Lane, you didn't—" Her heart gallops in her chest. "You don't have to do all this."

"Don't be silly." She sets out little containers of food; it's clear she made everything herself except for the champagne. "Sit."

They eat without talking much. It used to make her uncomfortable, sure that Lane's silence meant anger or judgement. But she's come to understand that it's just how Lane is: quiet, thoughtful, introspective. It's nice actually, that she can just be with Lane, not needing to fill the quiet spaces with meaningless patter or some reckless activity that gives them something, anything, to do. Lane takes neat, even bites of a sandwich and watches the tide go out. Willa is glad to see her back to her normal self.

"How are things with your parents?" Willa asks, once they've put the food away and stretched their legs out on the blanket.

Lane shrugs. "Oh, we're back to pretending nothing happened. That's how we handle difficult things in my family."

Willa winces. "Sorry."

"Oh, it's fine. Business as usual, really." Lane turns to face her, eyes squinted against the glare of the setting sun. "Are you wearing a bathing suit, by any chance?"

Willa plucks at her board shorts and pulls at the neck of her T-shirt to reveal the swimsuit top underneath. "In this weather? Always."

Lane bites her lip against a smile. "Want to go for a swim?"

CH. 39

THE WAVES ARE CALM AND tipped with gold, though still chilly enough to take Willa's breath away when a wave rolls by and splashes up against her waist. Lane, in a black cut-out one piece, takes her time, stepping forward then waiting until her body adjusts to the chill. Willa, however, dives right in, slipping below the water for long enough that Lane is calling her name when she breaks through the surface.

"What are you, part mermaid?" Lane paddles over, hair still dry.

She and her mom used to have breath-holding contests, hands clasped and legs churning as close to the sandy ocean floor as they dared, then racing back up to gasp and laugh and bob on the waves. The ocean is as comfortable to her as her own bed, so, "Yeah, maybe I am."

Lane smiles, then dips below a passing wave, coming back up with her hair plastered back, sleek and shiny and black as night. Willa treads water nearby.

"You're so lucky that you grew up here," Lane says. Her longer legs must touch the bottom; she's stable while Willa flips back to front, kicks her legs wildly, and swims in circles to stay afloat.

"Yeah, I am." She is glad to be here, truly, even when she sometimes yearns to be anywhere else.

A jogger passes by on the beach, sand flying behind them with each step. A group of teenagers tries and fails to ride boogie boards on the waves that peter out long before they hit the shore. Something slimy trails along Willa's foot, seaweed probably.

"You know, in some places the water is totally clear. Like you can see all the way down to the bottom," Willa says, plunging a hand below the opaque gray-blue water.

"Yes," Lane says. "I do know."

"You've been there," Willa guesses.

"Some. Not all of them."

"Not yet."

Lane acknowledges it with a tilt of her head. Stacked against Lane's experiences exploring the world, living in various places in between sailing jaunts, Willa is in a race she'll never finish, not even if Lane stands perfectly still for years. She loves this island, it's not just a place but a part of her, and yet…

"Do you ever feel like you're in a cage, and someone left the door open so you can leave any time you want, and then you just— don't."

A wave crests behind them, and they both swim up to rise over it. When they come back down, Lane is closer, close enough that Willa's feet and hands brush against her as she treads water. Lane's face is thoughtful, searching. The teenagers nearby scream and laugh.

"What if I leave," Willa says, "and nothing else out there can compare? What I leave, and it's awful?"

Lane reaches out, letting Willa cling to her so she doesn't have to keep fighting to stay afloat. She pushes water-logged curls from Willa's face and smiles softly. "Well, if the door is open… Why can't you just go back in if you need to?"

Willa doesn't answer. She's never thought about it like that. Lane's legs bracket Willa's; her arms are solid around Willa's waist. When Lane kisses her, it takes like the ocean. *I love you,* Willa thinks, to the rhythm of the waves cresting and falling and rushing to the shore. *I love you, I love you, I love you.*

Lane pulls back to whisper against Willa's lips, "Want to go inside?"

They stumble to the beach, hastily gather the picnic and their dry clothes, and shake out the blanket. Lane's apartment is freezing; the air-conditioning flicks goosebumps across their bare skin. Lane packed towels and hands one to Willa while Lane stands dripping on the floor mat in just her clinging suit. Despite the chill, Willa is already buzzing with anticipation; heat settles in her belly even as her teeth chatter. If Lane just wants to *show* Willa how she feels with sex, then Willa can be okay with that.

Lane's eyes slip low; her bottom lip is pinched between her teeth. She turns to Willa, slipping one bathing suit strap down and off her shoulder and then—

"We never did stay in and watch a movie like you wanted."

Lane's bare shoulder is so close she could put her mouth right on the smooth curve of it. *Wait. Did she just say watch a movie?*

Willa blinks. "Huh?"

Lane smiles in a way that suggests she knows exactly what she's doing. "I'm gonna go change, did you want something else to wear?"

"Um." Still trying to catch up with what's happening, Willa glances down at herself. The top and shorts are starting to dry. If she stands under the vent for a bit she should be good to go with just the towel folded beneath her. "I'm okay."

"Okay. The remote is on the table; you pick. I trust your judgement."

Willa stands there, blinking and cold, as Lane saunters off to get dressed. What is happening? And has anyone in her life ever said those words? "I trust your judgement." Willa rubs the towel over her face and is reasonably sure that the only appropriate response is to propose marriage to Lane, right here, in the soggy, cold foyer of her condo.

Or she could pick a movie.

"Ooh, good choice." Lane, now in a loose T-shirt and cotton shorts, plops onto the couch and tucks one leg beneath her. It's new, this relaxed version of Lane, and Willa wonders how many people get to see her like this. It feels like a privilege.

"You know this movie?" Willa drops the remote onto the coffee table and leans back. It's a new cult hit, one she thought she could introduce Lane to. The opening credits blare from the TV.

"Yes, Willa. I'm not totally hopeless with pop culture. Believe it or not, I was young once upon a time."

"I didn't mean like—" Willa frowns and watches the movie instead of protesting. She can't focus, though, and soon twists around on the couch to look at Lane. "It bothers you. The age difference." *If only you were ten years older.* Willa meant what she said, that she wouldn't hold anything Lane did or said when she was drunk against her. That doesn't mean she forgot.

Eyes on the TV screen, Lane replies, "I wish it didn't."

Willa allows the answer to hang there; both of them tune in to the movie and let the clock run out on the evening. But Willa soon loses focus on the plot. She doesn't want just something physical with Lane. She's not okay with going on the way they have, girlfriends in all but name because Lane is afraid of getting into a relationship and Willa is afraid to rock the boat. Hasn't Willa learned, through all that happened, to be honest despite the consequences? To go for what she wants instead of settling for what other people want her to be?

"It doesn't bother me," Willa says, loud over the music of a dramatic moment in the movie. "And it shouldn't bother you either. In fact, I think it's an excuse."

Lane's eyes narrow, and her chin lifts. "An excuse?"

"Yeah." Willa's mouth is getting ahead of her brain now, but for once she's not afraid of what will come blurting out. "Because I think you know how I feel about you and I think you feel the same way. But it scares you. So you pretend like this is some casual fling with someone too young for you to be serious about. And that's a lie. I can tell because I'm really good at lying."

The condo has grown dark and the TV flickers light and shadow on Lane's tightly held features. She doesn't give anything away, though

Willa knows she's gotten to her. In the movie, the main character hits their rock bottom moment, and Lane's head drops.

"What if—" she starts, voice low and tight. "What if we do this, and it ends badly? You, you're young. But I can't start all over, Willa. I can't— Not again."

And Willa would never hurt her, not on purpose, but she can't see into the future, either. She knows herself, too, her tendency toward impulse and deep-seated insecurities. She can't promise that they will never carelessly wound each other in a stupid fight or the heat of the moment.

"I think sometimes you have to take a chance and sail close to the wind." In sailing terms, that means to sail close-hauled, or to trim the sails tightly so that the boat can push into the wind as close as possible, so close that the sails are nearly horizontal, like a wing. In not-sailing terms, it means taking a risk, even when that seems foolhardy.

Lane dark eyes scan her face; reflected blue and yellow light flickers. "I don't know if I can."

 CH. *40*

WILLA DOESN'T STAY AFTER THE movie ends. She has more work to do on the cottage, needs to find a short-term housing solution for the summer, and has to find a new roommate for the fall. Plus, she has an important interview in the morning.

"Let me drive you home," Lane says. Willa nods and doesn't push Lane any further. If things are ever going to change between them, it's really up to Lane now.

The drive is quick and quiet. Lane pulls up in front of the cottage, putting the car into park next to the newly trimmed azalea bush on the curb. Willa's mom planted it when Willa was in elementary school. Back then it was just a spindly sapling stuck in the ground, and now it has grown so large that it's nearly consumed the entire mailbox; the bush is as wide as it is tall. "Bloom where you're planted," her mom would say when Willa had a tough day and refused to talk about what happened. Maybe she took that sentiment a little too far.

"Just you here right now?" Lane glances up the dark driveway. There's no bike or kayak or assorted outdoor gear in sight.

"Yeah, it's kind of weird. Though I was alone for a bit after my mom left and before Bodhi moved in." Willa releases her seatbelt and leans toward the door.

"Why did she leave?"

Willa pauses with her hand on the door handle. "Well. She fell in love, I guess."

"Ah," Lane says.

"I mean she'd have to really love him, right? To leave here and go to Missouri. I dunno. I don't get it, Tim's whole appeal. But I'm glad she's happy." She *is* glad. But Christina could have been happy here, was happy here. Willa cracks the door open, and the interior light pops on.

"Not a big fan of Tim?" Lane's face is amused and soft in the sudden bright light.

"No. I dunno. He and my mom met when I was teenager; like of course I wasn't gonna like him. He was dating my mom!" Tim first met Willa's mom when he was living on the island as an interim manager for a new hotel. Christina went in for an interview. She'd heard the pay was slightly better and the benefits much better there, and the rest is history. Or whatever. "He'd show up like, every night, with flowers or chocolate or a cheesy teddy bear. And he'd act like we were best buds, like right away he wanted to be my new dad, and it was way too much." Willa rolls her eyes at the memories. "How was school today kiddo?" he'd ask. Then he'd try to give her some sage advice and invite her to learn how to change the oil in a car. She's surprised he never suggested throwing a ball around out back.

"I guess it took me a long time to get over my first impression of him."

Lane smiles. "Yeah, I can understand that. Well. Good luck with your interview tomorrow."

"Thanks." Willa desperately wants to say something else. She wants, so badly, to give Lane some sort of ultimatum. "I'm in love with you," she'd say, "and we should be together and you know it" And Lane would kiss her and not say it back, but it wouldn't matter because Willa would know, without a doubt, that she felt the same. But what would change if she did?

She hops out of the car.

* * *

"Ms. Rogers, thank you for coming in. I must say, I'm impressed by your resume." Jenn and Robin snicker at the joke, pretending they've only just met, sitting across from Willa at the table where she's had countless meals and countless staff meetings that were really just the four of them, Jenn, Robin, Bodhi, and her, gossiping and laughing.

"Thank you for having me," Willa says, playing along. She's nervous, a little, though she shouldn't be. It's Robin and Jenn, who are essentially her second and third moms. She goes to their house for dinner. They buy her clothes. Once when she had the flu, they took her to the doctor, and Willa threw up on the floorboards of Jenn's car. Besides, no one knows this store the way she does. No one cares about this store as much as she does. She has this on lock. She tells Robin and Jenn as much. *On lock.*

"Here's the thing, Willa." The mood turns somber. Robin's face is drawn, and Jenn's hands are folded tight on the table. "The past five years you have been instrumental to the success of this store—"

"We couldn't have done it without you," Jenn adds.

"Your knowledge. Your customer service skills. Your can-do attitude—"

"A model employee."

"And a wonderful friend to our Bodhi—"

"The *best* friend."

Willa is starting to get whiplash going back and forth from Robin's serious expression to Jenn's matching one. Willa is starting to get the sense that this isn't going anywhere good.

"But…" Willa prompts.

Jenn sighs. She looks at Robin, who nods. "We don't think this is the right choice for you." Jenn unfolds her hands to reach for Willa's. Willa pulls her hand away.

"This is because I lied to you. About knowing how to sail."

"Willa, no."

"Not at all."

Willa shakes her head; tears burn behind her eyes. Of course it is, how could she have been so stupid? Why would they want a liar and fake to run their store? How could they trust her? And even though it's completely understandable and totally her own fault, anger flares in her chest.

"Then what?" she spits. "That guy that—rich asshole. He's better than me? He doesn't even live here! He isn't even from here! What does he know?"

"Willa," Robin says. The placating tone of her voice makes Willa realize she's been yelling. Willa looks down, ashamed.

"I'm sorry." Why can't she just *stop* and *think* sometimes?

"It's okay." Jenn reaches for her hand again, and this time Willa lets her take it. "It's okay to feel your feelings and be a human being with flaws."

Willa sniffles and nods. She mostly feels like a child. "Thank you for the opportunity," she mumbles and starts to push her chair back. This is what she gets for thinking she can be something more than what she is. For being real instead of faking it.

"Wait. Please."

When she first interviewed at the sail shop, she was desperate for Jenn and Robin to like her. They were so cool and chill, and their easy affection and commitment to each other and to the island and to Bodhi were like a drink of water after crawling through the desert. Willa, at eighteen, suddenly all alone and so unsure of herself, had a chance at a future. She had hope and people who were looking out for her. This store, Robin and Jenn and Bodhi, they saved her. All she ever wanted was to be worthy of that.

"Over the years," Robin starts, "We've come to think of you as another daughter." Willa has to swipe tears away. "And we have always raised Bodhi to be herself and go after the things that bring her joy. To…"

"Be free," Jenn fills in.

"You've done a great job because she definitely is *very* free." It's a jab at Bodhi and their parenting, but it's true. No one could ever accuse Bodhi of not following her bliss or being herself, no matter what.

"Yes, well. We always had faith she'd find a place to land eventually." Robin pats Jenn's hand and smiles reassuringly. How many sleepless nights did they spend, worrying that Bodhi would never figure out how to get to work on time, find a path, or settle down with someone. Or *someones*.

"And Willa, we want the same for you," Robin continues. "We have loved having you here, but this store, this little sail shop, it's not the end of your story."

"I don't—" Willa's glances back and forth, eyebrows furrowed. "I'm not sure I follow."

"We feel as if we would be doing you a disservice if we made you manager—"

"Not that you aren't qualified and not that we don't want you to be," Jenn cuts in.

"Exactly. There is so much more for you out there, Willa.

"So much life for you to live."

"This store was our dream. We just want you to have *your* dream."

Willa lets their words sink in. There's a dried blob of pasta sauce on the table that must be from the Chef Boyardee ravioli Bodhi had for lunch a few days ago. She scrapes it off with a fingernail.

"What if I don't know what my dream is?"

Jenn squeezes her hand. Robin takes the other one. "Then you go out and find it."

The job is hers if she wants it, they tell her. But they want her to really think about what they said, to take her time and be honest with herself. In a daze, head everywhere but in the present moment, Willa nearly walks right into Bodhi who is coming in as she goes out.

"Whoa, you okay?"

Willa frowns. "I don't know."

Bodhi glances inside, to where Robin and Jenn are still sitting at the table. "The moms got to you, huh?"

"Yeah. I guess so."

Bodhi grabs her shoulders as if to hold her upright. "Just remember, whatever they said, it comes from a place of love, okay? Also, sorry if it was weird."

"Love," Willa repeats. *Love. Go out and find it.* "I gotta go find Lane."

 CH. *41*

Lane isn't at work.

"You just missed her," the front desk assistant tells Willa, with a distressingly wide grin. She doesn't know where Lane is, the assistant answers when Willa asks, or, if she does, she certainly isn't telling Willa.

Lane isn't at home either, nor out on the beach. She's not at the yoga studio that shares space with an acupuncture clinic, not at The Oyster Bar or The Sand Dollar or any of the kitschy tourist stores or the regular ones people actually shop at. Willa finds herself back where she started, resting near the marina before she takes the long trip around to the other side of the island.

Then Lane's SUV pulls into the lot, and Willa pushes her board to the side of the road, letting it coast into a patch of sand as she jogs over.

"Hey."

"Willa, hey." Lane jumps a bit, surprised to see her. "How did your interview go?"

Willa, who was planning to confess her feelings in a rush the moment she saw Lane, isn't sure how to answer. "Um. Confusing?"

"Oh." Lane frowns. "Sorry."

"Yeah. I—" Willa shakes her head. "Actually, I wanted to talk to you about something."

Before Lane can respond, Mr. Kelley and his terrible nephew walk up.

"Ms. Cordova!" Mr. Kelley says. "She's all ready for you. I think you two will be very happy together." For a baffling second, Willa thinks he's talking about her and Lane, as if he somehow knew that Willa was looking for Lane to tell her that she loves her and wants to be with her and won't take "I can't" for answer. Then Mr. Kelley says, "Come see," and gestures toward the boats docked in the marina.

She is a boat.

"You bought a boat? You're sailing again?" Willa trails after the group; their footsteps patter discordantly on the dock. They all come to a stop at a boat painted white with a bold blue stripe on the hull. It's a Westsail, an older one, probably a thirty-two footer. It is, frankly, in terrible shape.

"I bought a boat," Lane says, cupping her hands over her eyes to inspect it. "Max helped me find it. Perfect, right?" Willa scowls instinctively. Of course Max helped her find it. Of course Lane likes him. But when did Lane buy a boat? And why didn't she say anything?

To Willa's unasked questions, Lane says, "I'd been thinking about it for a while. And after that dinner with my parents, I just thought, I dunno. Now or never I guess."

"Okay." Willa tries to pretend that Mr. Kelley and Mr. Kelley's irritating nephew aren't there. She moves around them to be closer to Lane. "I think it's great. I thought you would never sail by yourself again."

"Yeah, me too. I guess I just had to find the right reason. The joy of it." Lane got the same inspiring speech from Mr. Kelley, Willa guesses. Lane bites at her lip, uneasy about something.

"Well, that's great." Willa scans the boat again and tries to remember what she knows about the model. Built in the 1970s most likely, and someone—Max—has put in some upgrades. It's sturdy, despite its rough shape. It's probably not very fast and meant for, "Long-distance bluewater cruising," Willa murmurs, understanding settling on her shoulders. "You're leaving."

"That's the plan." A nervous glance again, which now makes sense. She was worried about telling Willa that she was leaving.

"What about your job?"

"I quit." She lifts her chin, obviously sure of this decision. "But not before I made my first and last sale." She smiles at Willa in a strangely secretive way. "Um," she looks over to Mr. Kelley and terrible Max. "If we could have a minute?"

A minute to say goodbye, Willa knows, so when Max says he wants to show Lane a few things on the boat really quickly, Willa is relieved that he's there. She's not ready to say goodbye. As Max shows them some repairs he made to the plumbing and gray-water system, new standing rigging, the solar panels, the brand-new, queen-size mattress in the hull, Willa also knows that she could never, ever be the person who asks Lane to stay.

Mr. Kelley and Max take Lane up to the deck for the rest of the tour. Willa sits in the kitchenette. It's a great boat or will be once it's fixed up a little more. Her hands itch to take a picture and post it, to pretend that this boat is hers and she knows exactly what to do next. Being herself has not been working out so great. There's a clatter of footsteps above deck, then the thunk of someone coming back down the little stairwell. Willa tries her best to look happy for Lane, who slaps a key down onto the table that is just big enough for two.

"What is this?" Willa loops the keyring onto her finger.

"A key. To your house." Lane sits and looks over at Willa with that same nervous glance.

"Okay…" She is not following. "Why?"

Lane nibbles on her lip. "Bodhi let me make a copy of her key. I guess I wanted something symbolic, but maybe the deed would have been better."

Willa scowls. What is this game? What the hell is Lane talking about? "The deed to *what*?" Willa says, not as patiently as she would like. She knows Lane has trouble communicating sometimes but she is totally lost here.

"Oh. Oh, gosh, I thought they would have told you by now." Willa waits, impatience still radiating from her. "You grandparents," Lane says. "Your mom and I convinced them to turn over the deed of the cottage. To you."

Willa stares at the key, silver and catching glints of sunlight through the portholes. It's something she never even thought to ask for, and not even something she's even sure she wants. The cottage is hers. Hers alone.

She presses the key into her palm; the teeth dig sharply into her skin. "I don't know what to say."

Lane looks at the table, traces the grain of the wood. Her dark hair is a glossy curtain falling just below her chin; her full lips are softly parted; her eyelashes are lush and full, casting shadows on her high cheekbones. In so many ways, she is the person Willa never saw coming, who crashed into her life like a rogue wave, sending her topsy-turvy and unsure which way was up. But she didn't change her; she made Willa feel that she was enough, just on her own, that she could do the things she wanted to do, instead of just pretending.

"You can rent it out," Lane says of the cottage. "If you want to. And I was hoping you might want to because—"

"I'm in love with you," Willa says, blurting it out before Lane can finish.

Lane looks up, smiles softly. "Because I was hoping you might want to come with me."

# CH. *42*

THERE'S A SPOT ON THE windowsill in the kitchen that's marred by scratches and nicks in the white paint. Willa's never bothered painting over it since it's usually covered by a row of fake potted flowers, but today she lifts the pots out of the way and begins to sand each mark smooth. There are random lines and crosses scrawled into the soft, flaking paint: her initials, a crooked smiley face, a *Willa was h,* a message she guesses wasn't finished because her mom fussed at her to stop. It brings her back to slow mornings, sitting up on the counter while her mom made banana pancakes with the sun bright and hot through the window and the day full of the sort of promise and freedom a childhood summertime can bring. She runs her fingertips over the words *Willa was h,* then scours them away.

She's just finishing the last corners and edges on the windowsill when someone knocks on the door. "Come in," she calls over the music, sets down her paintbrush, and turns the volume down on her phone with her non-paint-splotched hand. Charlie Cordova lets himself in.

"Looking good. Really coming along." Charlie has been to the house a few times already, first to survey the property, then to recommend ways to make the property more valuable, then taking pictures, then walking around with a home inspector. He looks quite a bit like Lane, perhaps predictably, given that Lane looks like their parents, who sort of look like each other. He's one of the top real estate agents on Porter

Island and has an easy sort of affability, all warm handshakes, easy smiles, and the kind of eye contact that makes people feel as if they're hanging on every word, as if everyone he speaks to becomes the most important person in the room.

"Came to update you," Charlie says, "We're in a three-way bidding war!"

Willa wishes Bodhi was here; she'd appreciate the snort Willa gives in response. "That's great, Charlie. And I trust you to squeeze every last penny out of whoever wins."

"Darn tootin'."

Ever since Willa decided not to take the cottage, she and Charlie have developed a casual comfortableness, though it was a little strange at first since she'd never met him.

"Lane and I haven't been close in a long time," he admitted when Willa brought it up while she was signing paperwork at his gleaming mahogany desk at the office. "She was the golden child, and I was the scapegoat. I was so jealous of her, until the tables turned. Now I don't envy that golden child status one bit. To be blunt, Willa. It sucks."

When Willa asked Lane about it, she just shrugged and said that was how it was. "We're both trying to break out of old patterns," she said.

In the cottage, Charlie looks around and whistles. "You're really sitting on a treasure here," Charlie says, folding his sunglasses and tucking them into the 'V' of his polo. "The location, the way it's been so well maintained, the fact that it's only ever had one owner in sixty years. The property value has skyrocketed. You sure you don't want to take ownership first and then sell?"

It's a question she asked herself over and over after Lane presented the opportunity to her a few weeks ago. It's tempting, but no. "I wouldn't feel right about it. My grandfather is having some significant health issues, and my grandmother hasn't been able to fully retire yet. It's wearing on her. Now they won't have to worry about it." She glances around the cottage, imagining every memory crammed invisibly into every square inch. "And anyway, it's time for me to move on. I think I finally realized that this place will always be part of me, no matter where I go."

"Lane doesn't mind me taking over then?"

"Lane recommended you." Charlie seems a little taken aback, but pleased. "Also, I love her, but she was a terrible realtor, and I think we all know it."

Charlie flashes one of his easy grins. "You love her?"

"I—" Willa flushes. "Yeah. I do."

Willa is still weighing whether she should go off with Lane on her sailing adventure or if she should first find her own path. What happens after the house sells, she doesn't know. What she'll do for work, she doesn't know either. But wherever Lane goes, with Willa or not, and no matter what dream Willa finds to chase down, she knows that love won't change.

"Well," Charlie says, plucking his sunglasses from his shirt. "I'm glad you love her, because she's put me in a bit of a bind."

"A bind?"

"It's just me at the office since she quit and the folks are gone. My property manager got poached by a different firm. Things are a little—" He twirls a finger around his ear and grimaces.

It's a lightbulb moment, an *of course* moment. No one knows this island as Willa does. No one loves it the way she does; no one else tucks every inch of it into their heart every single day. She knows how to sell things, how to find that perfect something for someone or deal with a picky, difficult customer with a smile on her face. And no one knows how to accentuate the positive by framing things just right quite the way she does.

"You know, Charlie," Willa says, walking him to the door with her own winning grin. "I had over five hundred thousand followers on Instagram at one point..."

*　*　*

"I CAN'T BELIEVE YOU'RE SO far away now," Willa whines. She tucks her chin over Bodhi's shoulder and pouts.

"Oh, my god, Wills. It's across the sound and south a little."

"*So far away*," Willa whines again. It feels like a million miles with Bodhi in Wilmington instead of sleeping in the room next to hers. They're at a tavern in downtown Wilmington, drinking fancy cocktails on a patio with a fire pit and a view of the Cape Fear River. It's a grown-up version of the beach bonfires at home, and Willa isn't sure she cares for it.

"You and Lane are going way farther, right?" Hunter asks. "If you go."

Willa makes a face. "We're not talking about me, *Hunter*."

Bodhi dislodges Willa from her shoulder and shakes her empty glass toward Hunter. "Babe, can you go get another one of these? Thank you." After she goes, Bodhi turns to Willa. "Is this about *me* leaving or about *Lane* leaving?"

Willa opens her mouth to say it's about Bodhi leaving, of course, and then starts to switch to admitting that it's actually about Lane leaving, but the truth, as she has been learning, lies somewhere in between. "It's like, all these things I've always wanted and thought I could never have and now that I do it's—"

"Terrifying?"

Willa breathes out with relief. "Yeah."

Here in the city, the nighttime is so much busier and brighter than on the island. Crowds of people pass on the cobblestone streets; snippets of loud conversation pass in and out; music pumps from speakers above them and carries, muted and thumping, across the street from a club. Smells from restaurants mix with cigarette smoke and car exhaust and the earthy scent of the river. What places could she and Lane sail to? Will they be loud and bustling or quiet and rural? Something new that Willa's never seen?

"Remember when you asked me once if it ever felt like I was just like, running in place?" Bodhi says with her eyes on Hunter as she weaves through the crowd with two fresh drinks. "I think we both were. But change is gonna come whether we want it to or not. Might as well embrace it. Besides, Wills, you're the bravest mofo I know."

Back on the island, the ferry will be finishing its last run and docking for the night. The beam from the lighthouse will soon sweep across the dark water. Willa's grandparents' house is sold, as of this afternoon. The sail shop is now in Max's hands. Many of their core group of friends are gone or making plans to be. It always seemed to Willa as if the island would stay the same forever, but of course it won't. Of course, it never did. Hunter and Bodhi wind themselves together on a couch, flirting with the guy who was already sitting there. Across the patio, Lane is chatting easily with Charlie, who came along to celebrate the big sale and Willa's new, very flexible, job as a property manager. Lane smiles and waves, and Willa's chest warms. She wonders sometimes what would have happened if she'd never run into Lane. What trajectory would her life have taken? Would she have been as unchanged as the ferry lumbering back and forth on its route? Perhaps searching endlessly across an empty ocean like the beam of the lighthouse? She thinks she would have gotten here somehow. Lane finally comes back, just as Hunter and Bodhi leave with their new companion.

"Ready?" Lane says.

"Ready," Willa answers.

EPILOGUE

THE SINK IS BACKING UP again. Not only is it just barely big enough to accommodate two sets of breakfast dishes—two bowls, two coffee mugs, four spoons—but whatever 1970s boat plumbing system it's been labyrinthed into makes it cough up the contents of the gray-water tank on a frequent, though random, basis.

"Did you flush the toilet too hard?" Lane asks, shirt pulled up to cover her nose. The odor is a forceful bouquet: sewage plus rotting food plus the chemical-sweet smell of the drain treatment they dump down it to keep the backups to a minimum.

"How would I even do that?" Willa replies through a plugged nose. "Like, aggressively flush a toilet? How would I go about doing that?"

"I don't know!" Lane drops the shirt covering half of her face to make a frustrated gesture with both hands, then grimaces at a fresh wave of stench hitting her anew. "Ugh."

Their options for dealing with a backed up sink while miles and miles out to sea are very few. Their options for dealing with each other while miles and miles out to sea on a thirty-two-foot-long sailboat with just under two hundred square feet of living space are even fewer. Willa squeezes herself into the cramped kitchen space, which is really just a two-burner stove, mini fridge, microwave and tiny sink boxed in by equally cramped cabinets, and grabs a cup to help Lane scoop the filthy, putrid water from the sink.

"I've got it." Lane grunts, elbow colliding with Willa's arm; the now-full cup splatters gray water across the counter. Willa curses and switches to cleaning off the counter.

"No, no. If you're gonna blame me, I'll do it. Everything is always my fault, right?"

"I'm not blaming you." Lane says, in a tone way too placating for Willa's liking. She dumps a cupful of dirty water into a bucket that they keep under the sink for exactly this purpose. Also, for sea sickness. "I was just thinking that maybe when you flushed the toilet, it caused the backup."

"Right, because I'm so incompetent I don't know how to flush a toilet!"

"Oh, my god, stop being so defensive!"

"You know what?" Willa spikes her plastic cup onto the counter and extricates herself from the tiny space. "Maybe you *should* do it yourself." She stomps across the cabin, up to the cockpit and out onto the deck, going all the way out to where the railing comes to a point at the very tip of the hull. She leans against it and looks out across the ocean, endless in all directions. It's as far as she can get from Lane right now, and the pit in her stomach makes her wish she wasn't. She could have helped Lane finish emptying the sink at least.

Willa is living her dreams, with the person of her dreams, so she should be nothing but happy. She's finding, though, that even a dream life can be messy. And sometimes it can smell like rotting sewage and drain cleaner.

Willa pulls her phone out and opens her new Insta account, and starts a livestream. In the camera, her hair is snarled in the wind, the skin on her shoulders is peeling and raw, but even she can see how bright her eyes are these days, how genuine her smile. "Hey all, so in my ongoing effort to keep things real with y'all—I'm sure you're all still having nightmares from the wicked sunburn I got in the Bahamas, use that sunscreen, kids!—things on the boat are not all paradise either, I assure you..."

She quickly details the sink, the struggles of sharing close space with someone, how hard it is missing everyone sometimes. When she signs off, Willa feels a lot better. The fight about the sink didn't really have much to with the sink, not really.

Before they left Porter Island, Lane worked on fixing up the boat and gave sailing lessons all summer and through the fall while Willa got the hang of her new job as property manager and realtor-in-training at the Cordova family real estate firm. So when they took sailing trips together, it was an overnight here, a weekend there, never farther than a ways up or down the East Coast, never long enough to get on each other's last nerve. This is the tail end of three months, December through February, after they sailed south and east to the places Willa had always wanted to see. And now she's seen the crystal clear waters and the white sand beaches and the calm brown water of the gulfs. She was surprised but pleased to find that no matter what it looks like, ocean waves sound just the same when she closes her eyes. No matter how far they've sailed, she recognizes it. Deep in her soul, she *knows* it.

"Hey," Willa says, ducking down the stairs and finding Lane in the very back of the cabin, cross-legged on the bed, as if she was also trying to get as far away as possible. The smell has been contained somewhat, and, when Willa closes the vinyl panel that sections off the bed from the rest of the cabinet in lieu of an actual door, it only smells a little terrible.

"Hey." Lane fiddles with the cowrie shell bracelet they bought in Port Lucaya. "Sorry."

"No, I'm sorry." Willa shuffles over on her knees. There's only space for a bed, one just barely big enough for the two of them, and overhead cabinets that they've stuffed to the brim. "I was being defensive." Willa sits cross-legged, too, and takes Lane's hand.

"Well, I was blaming you," Lane says, fiddling with Willa's fingers.

"Yeah. Maybe I do flush the toilet too aggressively though."

Lane's frown tips up into a wry smile, and she lifts their joined hands to press her lips to Willa's knuckles. "I think I'm ready to go home."

Willa has worried a lot about how they would make this work long-term. They haven't talked about it because Willa hasn't wanted to know the answer. Being with Lane, exploring all these new places, being a team and sailing the boat together, it's been enough. But Willa has a job to get back to, family and friends-turned-family she misses. Lane, however, sold her condo and quit her regular job and still has a strained, if slightly improved relationship with her family. If Porter Island is an open cage that allows Willa to flit back and forth as she pleases, then what is it to Lane? A tether to a place she doesn't want to be and people she'd rather leave behind, or so Willa had worried.

"You think of it that way?" Willa unfolds her legs and pats the mattress. Sometimes it's easier for Lane to talk if they aren't directly face-to-face. "Home?"

Lane tucks herself into Willa's chest, sighs as Willa wraps her arms tightly around her. "I never thought I'd say this, but yeah. I think I do."

Willa breathes against her silky hair and smells salt and coconut shampoo and the slight lingering odor of the backed-up gray-water tank. "What changed?"

Lane is still uncomfortable with emotions, still struggles with vulnerability. Willa, for that matter, is still prone to act first and think later, to scrutinize herself and come up wanting. But what Lane feels for her, how she feels with Lane, that's no longer a question. It's there every time they kiss, and in the way Willa catches Lane looking at her when she thinks Willa isn't looking back; it's evident in the way Willa wakes every morning with Lane's arms and legs twined over her body, as if Lane was afraid Willa might disappear while she's sleeping. Lane's feelings for her are there in every meal she cooks for Willa in the tiny kitchen, and when they're docked and go their separate ways to explore, she can see Lane's true feelings in the way her eyes light up when they find each other again, her excitement in telling Willa what she saw and did and bought. She knows how Lane feels about her, and yet, when Lane turns in her arms and looks in her eyes and says, "Well, I guess I fell in love," Willa's heart is suddenly too full to fit in her chest and she has to kiss Lane just so she can breathe again.

"I love you too," Willa says and rests their foreheads together.

"How about you?" Lane asks after a while. "Are you ready to head home?"

"Yeah," Willa says, though it's not entirely true. She is anxious to get back to Porter Island and find some solid ground, but she doesn't think of Porter Island that way anymore. Because as long as she has the ocean and Lane, she's always home.

THE END

ACKNOWLEDGMENTS

THANKS, AS ALWAYS, TO MY patient and supportive family. To Annie, Candy, and Choi for still believing in me and still pushing me. Finally, growing up queer in the South for me means having a complicated relationship with the idea of home. Of loving a place but knowing it doesn't always love you back, at least, not the real you. Like Willa, I learned to hide parts of myself and fake it just to get by, and also like Willa, I could only do that for so long. This is the first story I've written that is set in my home state and even though there will always be a part of me that yearns to leave, North Carolina is stitched into my heart and always will be. So thank you for being my home and for giving me so many people I love, and for being the place where I learned to love myself.

ABOUT THE AUTHOR

LILAH SUZANNE IS A QUEER author of bestselling and award-winning romantic fiction. Their 2018 novel *Jilted* was named a finalist for a Lambda Literary Award and a Foreword INDIES Award and won a Bisexual Book Award for romantic fiction. Their critically acclaimed Spotlight series included the Amazon #1 bestseller *Broken Records*, along with *Burning Tracks* and *Blended Notes*. Lilah also authored the romantic comedy *Spice*, the novellas *Pivot & Slip* and *After the Sunset*, and the short story "Halfway Home," from the holiday anthology *If the Fates Allow*. A writer from a young age, Lilah resides in North Carolina and mostly enjoys staying indoors, though sometimes ventures out for concerts, museum visits, and quiet walks in the woods.

interludepress™

🌐 interludepress.com
🐦 @InterludePress
📘 interludepress
🛒 store.interludepress.com

interlude press
also by Lilah Suzanne...

Broken Records
Spotlight Series, Book One

Los Angeles-based stylist Nico Takahashi loves his job—or at least, he used to. Feeling fed up and exhausted from the cutthroat, gossip-fueled business of Hollywood, Nico daydreams about packing it all in and leaving for good. So when Grady Dawson—sexy country music star and rumored playboy—asks Nico to style him, Nico is reluctant. But after styling a career-changing photo shoot, Nico follows Grady to Nashville where he finds it increasingly difficult to resist Grady's charms.

ISBN (print) 978-1-941530-57-3 | (eBook) 978-1-941530-58-0

Burning Tracks
Spotlight Series, Book Two

In the sequel to *Broken Records*, Gwen Pasternak has it all: a job she loves as a celebrity stylist and a beautiful wife, Flora. But as her excitement in working with country music superstar Clementine Campbell grows, Gwen second-guesses her quiet domestic bliss. Meanwhile, her business partner, Nico Takahashi and his partner, reformed bad-boy musician Grady Dawson, face uncertainties of their own.

ISBN (print) 978-1-941530-99-3 | (eBook) 978-1-945053-00-9

Blended Notes
Spotlight Series, Book Three

Grady Dawson is at the top of his music career and planning his wedding with boyfriend Nico when his past shows up, news of his nuptials is leaked, and his record company levels impossible demands. Can he make the ultimate choice between a private life with Nico and the public demands of his career?

ISBN (print) 978-1-945053-23-8 | (eBook) 978-1-945053-40-5

Jilted

Finalist, 2018 Lambda Literary Awards

In Lilah Suzanne's new romantic comedy, Carter, a weary architect, and Link, a genderqueer artist, bond over mutual heartbreak when their respective exes run off together. Against the eclectic and electric backdrop of New Orleans, Carter and Link have to decide if a second chance at love is in the cards.

ISBN (print) 978-1-945053-64-1 | ISBN (eBook) 978-1-945053-65-8

"Halfway Home"

An Interlude Press Short Story featured in If the Fates Allow

Avery Puckett has begun to wonder if her life has become joyless. One night, fate intervenes in the form of a scraggly dog shivering and alone in a parking lot. Avery takes him to a nearby shelter called Halfway Home where she meets bright and beautiful Grace, who is determined to save the world one stray at a time.

ISBN (print) 978-1-945053-47-4 | ISBN (eBook) 978-1-945053-48-1

"After the Sunset"

An Interlude Press Short Story

Caleb Harris and Ty Smith-Santos have never crossed paths until they learn that a farm in Sunset Hallow, Washington has been bequeathed to both of them. They prepare to sell the farmhouse, but soon find themselves falling for the charming farm, the lonely man who left it to them, and each other..

ISBN (eBook) 978-1-945053-49-8

Spice

In his Ask Eros advice column, Simon Beck has an answer to every relationship question his readers can throw at him. But in his life, the answers are a little more elusive—until he meets the newest and cutest member of his company's computer support team. Simon may be charmed, but will Benji help him answer the one relationship question that's always stumped him: how to know he's met Mr. Right?

ISBN (print) 978-1-941530-25-2 | (eBook) 978-1-941530-26-9

Pivot and Slip

Former Olympic hopeful Jack Douglas traded competitive swimming for professional yoga and never looked back. When handsome pro boxer Felix Montero mistakenly registers for his yoga for Seniors class, Jack takes an active interest both in Felix's struggles to manage stress and in his heart and discovers along the way that he may have healing of his own to do.

ISBN (print) 978-1-941530-03-0 | (eBook) 978-1-941530-12-2